SHINING WANDERER

by

ROSE ELVER

HARLEQUIN BOOKS

TORONTO
WINNIPEG

Original hard cover edition published in 1975
by Mills & Boon Limited

SBN 373-01949-1

Harlequin edition published February 1976

Printed in Canada

A
Harlequin
Romance

WELCOME

TO THE WONDERFUL WORLD

OF *Harlequin Romances!*

Interesting, informative and entertaining,
each Harlequin Romance portrays an appealing
and original love story. With a varied array
of settings, we may lure you on an African safari,
to a quaint Welsh village, or an exotic riviera
location — anywhere and everywhere that adventurous
men and women fall in love.

As publishers of Harlequin Romances, we're
extremely proud of our books. Since 1949,
Harlequin Enterprises has built its publishing
reputation on the solid base of quality and
originality Our stories are the most popular
paperback romances sold in North America; every
month, eight new titles are released and sold at
nearly every book-selling store in Canada and the
United States

A free catalogue listing all available Harlequin Romances
can be yours by writing to the

HARLEQUIN READER SERVICE,
(In the U.S.): M.P.O. Box 707, Niagara Falls, N.Y. 14302
(In Canada): Stratford, Ontario, Canada. N5A 6W4

or use order coupon at back of books.

We sincerely hope you enjoy reading
this Harlequin Romance.

Yours truly,

THE PUBLISHERS
Harlequin Romances

CHAPTER ONE

JASSY LANYARD saw the first of the islands through a breaking drift of cloud, surfacing like an emerald in the Indian Ocean. A heavy swell foamed into white smoke and spread in thick whorls of froth along the reefs, as though the emerald was set on blue silk with a flounce of white lace.

As the executive jet banked and circled she glimpsed a secluded bay; limpid water bobbing with boats, sands and white walls, splashes of vivid colour and dark fibre-thatch. And then acres of palm trees soaring to meet them, line upon line, like a regiment of green mop-heads drawn up in rows.

The airstrip was little more than a clearing surrounded by green, perched on the northern tip of the island above the pounding breakers. A dazzling white runway unravelled in a ribbon under the wheels as they touched down and Jassy held her breath because, for good or ill, it was over. The aircraft bumped gently as it taxied in. The whine of the engine died.

Dabbing the shine off her nose, shaping her mouth with a soft lipstick, Jassy reassured herself again and again that she had a right to be here. "This is your home," the letter had said, "and you're welcome to visit us or live here if you so choose. But think it over carefully. It's a long, tiring journey, and you will probably find it difficult to adapt yourself to such an isolated place after the sort of life you've been leading."

5

The letter had been short to the point of incivility, written in a firm black scrawl and signed without any conventional courtesies : "Ben Lanyard".

Mr Chandra clicked the catches shut on his attaché case and rose from his seat. Jassy could hear one of the pilots shouting something from the cockpit to someone outside. She peered from her window but could see only the empty airstrip. They must be on the other side, she thought, hastily pushing her odds and ends into her carry-bag with trembling fingers. Steps rattled as the door of the plane opened, and Mr Chandra said politely : "Please to go first, Miss Lanyard."

Jassy paused at the door, hesitating, pulling the straw handles of the carry-bag over her arm. Now that she had arrived she would have given anything to be able to turn her back on it all, close her eyes and open them again in London. What if the Lanyards of the Suran Islands resented her intrusion—breaking into their own separate little world? She did not know them, or even much about them. She had never seen them, nor they her, and she knew nothing at all about life in the islands and the running of the Lanyard Estates. But she was a Lanyard and she had her rights too—which included coming and finding out for herself.

If they resented it, she would have to try and show them that she had not come to interfere but to learn. As far as she was concerned it was to be something of a holiday—at least for the present—and she asked for nothing more than the hospitality any other visitor would get. But how did one explain all this on paper to a stranger who wrote a brusque invitation that seemed to say "come if you must, and let's get it over with as soon as possible".

There was a large man holding the steps at the door, extending a large brown hand to steady her. He wore a khaki shirt and shorts and a neatly-wrapped turban with a brass badge pinned on it. He would have looked very official if it had not been for the flash of white teeth smiling at her through a bushy black beard, and a pair of eyes wrinkling in friendly curiosity.

Jassy smiled back with all the assurance she could muster and went down the steps into this strange new world, drenched in hot sunlight.

The small concrete apron of the airstrip was empty too and the anticlimax was quite a blow. Nobody to meet her?—no welcome at all? She stood beside the plane, unsure of what was to happen next. Apart from the turbanned man holding the steps the only people she could see were three or four Suran islanders, their copper-skinned, muscular torsos bare to the sunshine, coming towards the plane from a cluster of palm huts. There was no one waiting on the tufted grass and no car to be seen on the roadway of crushed white coral that skirted the field and disappeared into the distant line of palm trees.

In the background, the verandah of a long, white-washed control building was dark with shade; not a sign of movement, although when she glanced up she thought she glimpsed a face at one of the windows of the small turret. Beyond the control block loomed a corrugated-iron hangar topped with a mast on which a bleached wind-sock flapped and billowed in the brisk, salty breeze.

Jassy had not expected to be greeted with open arms.

7

She hardly knew what to expect—a rather stiff, awkward reception, perhaps. But *this*? It left her feeling a bit apprehensive, marooned in the middle of nowhere.

She turned with some relief to Mr Chandra as he came out of the plane. He stooped a little as he took each step, with his attaché case clutched in one hand, his topee tucked under his arm and the sun glinting on the bald brown dome of his head fringed with hair as white as his spotless cotton jacket.

"Is this Heena?" Jassy asked tentatively, putting her pink straw beach hat and sun-glasses on.

"No, this is Sura island," he told her. "Heena is on the other side of the lagoon." His eyes, blinking behind gold-rimmed spectacles, were shrewd but immensely kind. "Do not fear, Miss Lanyard! The aeroplane has made such good time that we are much more early than expected. Otherwise Mister Ben and Miss Betty would have been here by now. The pilot has radioed and they will come soon. No more than half an hour or so. You do not mind?"

"Of course not." Jassy was perversely relieved that the moment for meeting them could be postponed a little while longer. She had braced herself for it during the flight, but she was glad of a breathing space to adjust to the strangeness of it all. The bareness, the stillness, the heat beating on her arms.

"This is Elahi, our postmaster," said Mr Chandra. "He comes to take the mail-bag."

"That is my duty," said the turbanned man, nodding cheerfully, "but today is es-special for me, being the first to see you here from England."

"Thank you." Jassy warmed to his broad smile. He

at least had been early enough to meet the plane and seemed glad of her arrival.

"Come to the verandah out of the sun," Mr Chandra suggested. "You would like some tea—no?"

"I would love a cup of tea—yes!" said Jassy.

"No worry for your luggage," he said. "It will all be done."

It *had* all been done for her ever since the tall, thin, stooping figure of Mr Chandra had met her at Santa Cruz airport in Bombay where he had introduced himself with grave courtesy, explaining that he had been sent to escort her to the Suran Islands, apologising because "Mister Ben" and "Miss Betty" had not been able to come themselves.

He had accompanied her on the flight to Colombo, installed her in the best hotel and presented himself promptly the next morning to board the Lanyard aircraft for the last stage of the journey. Her hotel bill had been paid, the luggage assembled, the car ready at the door. Jassy had only to sit back and relax. Lanyard's had their own aircraft for freight and mail to and from the Islands, with a Canadian pilot and Suran co-pilot, ready to fly them out again.

Beyond the Lacadive and Maldive islets came banks of cloud in the endless distance and the Indian Ocean far below caught in folds of light like a sheet of steel-blue silk spread over the whole world. A smiling Suran boy called Billy served "tiffin", a delicious chicken curry and rice followed by mango fruit and iced coffee. Mr Chandra had provided Jassy with a selection of magazines, but she had been too taken up with a mounting glow of hope and anticipation.

And now? Nothing but a dull, uneasy sense of

9

anticlimax.

As she walked along the pathway of crushed coral beside Mr Chandra, glancing around at the deserted airstrip thousands of miles from everything she knew, she wondered with a sinking heart if Ben Lanyard had deliberately planned this to make her feel unwelcome; trying to warn her that he was none too pleased. A man absorbed in the closed community he lived in, impatient of strangers, even a stranger who bore his own name and had a right to be here.

A dusty loofah-vine hung on the low picket fence edging the patchy grass of the control block. Along the plinth of the building little clumps of bronze marigolds shone against the flaking whitewash. Jassy followed Mr Chandra on to the verandah where some wicker chairs and a table had been set out among the pools of sunlight and shade so that she could wait in comfort.

She pulled off her floppy straw hat and tried to relax. Billy came staggering up the path with his tiffin basket, dumping it on the edge of the verandah for a moment with a breathless grin.

"Bring tea," said Mr Chandra as the boy heaved up the basket and disappeared into the building. "Where there is English or Indians or Chinese there will always be good tea!" He seemed almost jovial as he sank into a chair.

Jassy sat looking at the plane out there in the glare of the strip, and tried to think about the final stage that would eventually get her to the island of Heena. The whole journey from London was becoming unreal, like a dream in a haze of heat; the humid heat of Bombay and Colombo that had made her feel lifeless; the hypnotic fans endlessly spinning round. It was hot here too, but a different kind of heat. The sunshine was just as brilliant but not so cruel. She took off her sun-glasses and slipped them into her bag.

The Surans were squatting in the shade of the plane and one of the pilots stood leaning casually at the door, his cap tipped back, talking to the postmaster. They were all waiting, as she was having to wait, grateful for the salty wind off the reefs that cooled the sweat on their skins. They were all waiting for Ben Lanyard . . . as if he had stopped the world to suit himself.

Jassy asked: "Is it far to Heena Island?"

"Not far now," said Mr Chandra reassuringly. "We are at Sura North Point. Eight miles to Sura Main Bay, and three miles across the lagoon. No doubt you are feeling tired?"

"No, not that. It's just that I don't know much about the Suran Islands."

"Ah, well." Mr Chandra tucked his attaché case and topee away under his chair. "There are many groups of oil islands in this ocean. Ours is Sura Atoll —Sura, Heena, Miro, Venda and St George. Then there are also four outer coral islands, on reefs, you know? Very dangerous to go there because of the reefs. They have coconut plantations only, no houses. They are called The Sisters."

"Heena is the island where the Lanyards live?"

"Their house is on Heena, that is so. But these island are . . . how shall I tell you . . . like a family. Each one is separate, but each is part also of all the others. For many generations the house of the Lanyards was at Sura Main Bay. About sixty years ago they built on Heena and gave the place at Main

Bay to the village. It is our biggest village now, the capital of the islands, and the house is a guest-house. Mr Calver, our pilot, is living there now, and Dr Ducase, and Mr Jimmy who is manager of the factories."

"Factories?" She was surprised, thinking about machinery and smoky chimneys. "Out here?"

"Certainly," he smiled a little, "but not as you would know. It is the old meaning—factory—for copra, oil and spices. Coconut, cinnamon, nutmegs. You will see. You will visit. For a Lanyard all the islands are important."

"Does Mr Lanyard control everything?"

"Of course. It is his privilege. And his duty to us, which he would never fail. There is also an Advisory Council—he insists on that."

She had imagined, if she had thought about it at all, that Lanyard Estates was just a business on the islands, run like any other company. It suddenly dawned on her that there was a great deal more involved—the whole community of the islands, its government, its people. Was it all in Ben's hands?

"It is in the blood, no?" said Mr Chandra. "The Lanyards have had grant of the islands since the time of Captain Harry Lanyard who was with the great Captain Cook. Two hundred years gives many privileges, but responsibilities too." Pausing, he said. "Your name is Jacynth, eh? Made Jassy for short?"

. "That's right," she smiled in surprise.

"Like your grandmother. I knew her well—also your father." He sighed. "It was a great sorrow to us when that motor crash killed your parents."

"I can hardly remember them," she admitted

slowly. "I was only about four years old when it happened."

The change had come so abruptly and was so bewildering that she could recall very little, except being hurriedly washed and dressed by Mrs Pinkerton the housekeeper, white-faced with shock, and carried off from her home in Surrey to a tall grey house in a London square. After that she had cried incessantly for her mother and father until she gradually learnt that they would not be coming to fetch her and that "Aunt Dora" and "Uncle Cecil" had taken their place, with Mrs Pinkerton to fuss over her solitary childhood.

Indirectly, piece by piece, the meaning of it all had reached Jassy through the conversations of Aunt Dora and the sympathetically inquisitive ladies who came to coffee parties or afternoon tea.

Jassy would be brought to the drawing-room by Mrs Pinkerton, and Aunt Dora would beckon her forward: "Come here, Jacynth, and say how-do-you-do." And then significantly, in a lower tone: "The Lanyard child. Such a tragic business. I had to take her at once. There was no one else to cope."

The phrases overheard by the shy, sensitive little girl, sitting primly on the edge of a chair, had always remained in her mind. "Her mother had no people and Sura was out of the question. . . . The Suran Islands, in the Indian Ocean—quite impossible! . . . No, I'm not sure. Southwards from the coast of Ceylon, I think. South of the Equator. . . . Well, we have to consider her education, and there are other problems. . . ."

Mr Chandra was saying: "You have lived with your relatives?"

"No," she said, "not relatives. They were my guardians."

She could remember Aunt Dora making it clear to everyone right from the start. "Oh no, no connection with our family. No relation at all really. Jacynth is Cecil's ward. He used to handle Tom Lanyard's affairs and he's looking after Jacynth's interests until she comes of age."

Jassy had soon become used to being called "Jacynth" because Aunt Dora disapproved of shortening names and nicknames. She was an austere lady who belonged to several well-meaning committees and had a domestic and social routine that must not be disturbed. She took a pride in Jassy's appearance and good manners, sent for a doctor at the first sign of a rash or temperature, approved Mrs Pinkerton's harsh notions on discipline, and chose the schools to which Jassy was sent. She had no time to spare for play or confidences or loving.

Her brother, Uncle Cecil, had had a kindly manner but was completely preoccupied with his legal work. He drove away in the mornings, looking like an industrious mole, deep in the polished leather of a large black limousine. He was frequently away on cases, and the weekends he was at home Jassy had strict instructions not to make a noise as he was working in his study. Jassy was vaguely aware that he took an interest in her well-being, but he neither understood nor felt at ease with children and accepted Dora's opinions and decisions without question.

It would not have occurred to him that Jassy was unhappy; and the truth was that she had always had everything she needed—except a sense of belonging, of having someone of her own. She had merely been "Cecil's ward" and "the Lanyard child", and it described exactly her position in the household. After Aunt Dora's oblique references to the Lanyards of the Suran Islands in the early days she hardly ever mentioned them again, and they had disappeared into the recesses of Jassy's memory, like names in a story-book, too unreal to have any place in her life.

When she went away to boarding school Mrs Pinkerton had retired and severed Jassy's last link with her childhood. From then on she was on her own, as isolated and stubbornly independent as she could be. Not to be a burden to Aunt Dora and Uncle Cecil, who had had to provide so much for the Lanyard child already, became a matter of pride. And if you made no demands on others and did not expect much you did not get hurt. Loneliness, Jassy soon found, was less pain than being rebuffed.

"They were good to you, these guardians?" Mr Chandra enquired gently.

"Oh, yes. But I couldn't impose on them indefinitely. I've managed on my own for the last three years. I'm afraid they think I'm foolish and obstinate!"

"Then you take after your father, Miss Jassy," nodding and crinkling his mouth in amusement. "Even when a small boy he was a most stiff-necked and stubborn child if he set his mind. May-lee will tell you the same."

At this moment Billy reappeared on the verandah with the tea tray which he set on the wicker table in front of Jassy.

"Please to start," Mr Chandra bowed with old-fashioned courtesy towards the tray.

As she poured the tea and passed Mr Chandra his cup she reflected that she didn't like the idea of being thought stubborn; it smacked of unreasonableness. Independent, yes—she had had to be that, facing up to the fact that she was virtually alone in the world, finding it more and more irksome to have to accept the Winworthys' charity.

At eighteen she was at last free to stand on her own feet, but it had been a struggle. Matching Aunt Dora's rigid disapproval with quiet insistence, she had moved into a flat with one of her old school friends, put her whole mind into qualifying as a secretary and got herself a job on a magazine. She had worked hard, refusing to touch the allowance Uncle Cecil kept on paying into her bank account because she felt she had no right to the money. She had also tried desperately hard to keep up with all the fleeting crazes the other girls enjoyed, but the life they led cut right across the grain of her reserved, rather solitary background. As the months went by the endless succession of noisy parties and superficial relationships began to wear her down. She was too sensitive, too innately shy for the casual affairs her new circle of friends took so lightly.

Then she had fallen in love with Toby Taylor . . . just thinking about it was an agony of mortification and despair.

Toby could turn on the charm to persuade any girl his roving fancy chose that she was the most desirable woman he knew. Jassy had been given all the gossip about his love 'em, take 'em, leave 'em reputation. How could she have been so stupid and naïve as to imagine it would be different in her case? His glib assurances, his persistence, that endearingly boyish smile that somehow never lighted his eyes—she should have known!

She had been strongly attracted to Toby from the start, and the simple joy of feeling loved and wanted for the first time in her life gradually overcame her doubts about him. Her response was cautious, shy and gentle, but her longings went deep. One evening, before things had gone too far, she had overheard the brutal truth. Toby had nicknamed her "Miss Prude" and taken a bet with his cronies that he could seduce her easily. He had put money on it.

The realisation sickened her. She had pleaded a headache and left the party without a word to him or anyone else. She became cool and elusive again, covering the wounding experience with a shell of detachment, and Toby Taylor, who had lost his bet and been made to look foolish, never forgave her.

To forget Toby was another matter—it would be impossible to forget the blow to her impulsive and desolate heart. But she had learnt a lesson and would never allow herself to be so foolishly vulnerable again.

Soon after her twenty-first birthday she had been summoned to Cecil Winworthy's City office where he had explained that under the terms of her father's will there were now official papers to be signed. She had sat opposite him in a large, imposing room lined with law books, listening as he outlined the terms of the will under which she had become the owner, in her own right, of one-third of the shares in Lanyard Estates in the Suran Islands.

It meant very little to her. Her face was expressionless, her eyes tired and shadowy. He said in his precise but kindly way: "You're looking thin, not at all well,

Jacynth. You should have stayed with us and gone to college, you know. The lives you young people lead these days. . . ." He broke off, shaking his head, pursing his mouth judicially. Then out of the blue: "Why don't you go home for a while, Jacynth? Get away from all the pressures here and have a quiet holiday. I can write to your kinsman, Ben Lanyard, and tell him that as you now hold your father's rights and shares in the Suran Islands you will join them at Heena, to have a look at the Estates. You can afford to go."

For an instant the word "home" had caught her heart; but the Suran Islands were an unknown, alien world. He might as well have suggested that her home was on the moon. And yet it was a spark, setting her interest alight. An unexpected way out. Travelling across the world, meeting new people, perhaps even finding her own place, her roots. The Suran Islands! —she remembered now.

Still she hesitated. He said, almost sternly: "It would help you to get this—er—man off your mind. Make a new start, Jacynth."

She was startled out of her lethargy. How does he know it's a man, she wondered wryly, do I look so lovelorn? The colour surged to her face. He couldn't know about Toby. He was just guessing, that was all.

She said stiffly: "I don't think I should foist myself on the Lanyards."

"It's scarcely a question of their convenience. You're entitled to visit the islands, even live there if you wish. Shall I arrange it for you?"

Jassy, independent as ever, answered primly: "Thank you, Uncle Cecil, but I'd rather write to Mr

18

Lanyard myself. I owe them that at least."

That awkward letter of hers!—inviting herself to stay with strangers; and Ben's abrupt, far from cordial reply. Unconsciously she sat up straighter.

Well, it was too late to change her mind now. And perhaps it was too early to start regretting her decision to come to the islands.

She sipped the cup of hot, sweet tea and it was good. Why a hot drink should seem so good in a hot climate was a mystery! Tea, and talk, and the lazy heat, and the group lounging easily by the plane out on the strip had encouraged her to relax, as if time itself was standing still for a while.

Mr Chandra had somehow become the reassuring centre of this strange homecoming. Home! Coconut palms ... manioc bushes ... the sea roaring on the reefs. ...

She said: "Before I go off to Heena, I'd like to thank you for taking care of me. You've been very kind. ..."

"No need to mention it, no need," he broke in, embarrassed, removing his spectacles to polish them with a large handkerchief and then putting them on again and carefully adjusting the thin gold loops behind his ears. "Ahh! Mr Calver will want some tea now."

Jassy looked across to the plane and saw the Canadian pilot striding over the tarmac to join them on the verandah; a broad, genial man in his early thirties with webs of humour on his face ingrained in the deep tan of the tropics.

"We didn't have time to get acquainted this morning," he greeted her, engulfing her hand in his.

"No. Would you like some tea, Mr Calver?"

"The name's Ray."

"Mine's Jassy."

"Welcome home. Sorry I've been so long." He dropped comfortably into one of the chairs and the wicker creaked under his sturdy frame. "Straight as it comes, Jassy. No milk."

She poured him a cup.

Putting some papers and a tin of cigarettes on the table, he said: "All clear, Chan. We've sorted the Heena stuff from the rest. D'you think it's safe to get it out on the tarmac now?"

Mr Chandra returned his cup to the tray, consulted his watch and went to the edge of the verandah. After looking out for a moment he said thoughtfully: "No hurry."

"Okay. We don't want to get anything soaked." Ray Calver lifted an arm and signalled out to the plane. The Surans signalled back.

What on earth could get soaked here?—except with sunshine, Jassy wondered, looking at the tan of Ray Calver's bare arms and throat, brown as seasoned wood against his short-sleeved, open-necked white shirt.

Mr Chandra extracted his attaché case and topee from under his chair and tucked the documents Ray had given him into the case.

"Will you excuse, please, Miss Jassy? I must see the operator upstairs. He cannot leave the wireless room when he is doing duty. Mr Ray will keep company with you."

"Sure, leave her with me, Chan. It'll be a pleasure," Ray said.

"No need to ask if Chan's been looking after you," he commented as the old man disappeared through a door behind them. "Lanyard is the password around these parts. You're a cousin or something?"

"Or something," she said. "My father, Tom Lanyard, and Ben's father, John Lanyard, were cousins." Pride prevented her adding that Mr Chandra had had to explain the relationship to her.

"Ramu and the boys have been itching to come over and meet you, but they'll wait their turn."

"Whatever for?" she queried. "I mean, what's stopping them?"

"Etiquette, Jassy. The rule says your own folks have first call. Elahi jumped the gun when we arrived, but he had a cast-iron excuse!"

"Oh dear . . . I'm afraid I don't know any of the rules here."

He grinned. "Don't let it worry you. You'll soon get wised up. There's been talk, talk, talk about you ever since it was all fixed that you were coming. They'll be ferrying in from the islands to meet you, look you over."

"I hope I won't be a disappointment," she said lamely, controlling the shyness that made her gasp a little at this new notion. Meeting the Lanyards has so possessed her mind and the Sura airstrip had been so deserted that she had not thought of this—Tom Lanyard's daughter facing Tom Lanyard's Surans.

"Disappointment?" His face wrinkled engagingly. "A gorgeous gal like you? You're a celebrity already!"

She met his eyes. "Ray," she said suspiciously, "you're joking, aren't you?"

"Not on your life! It's a great day for them in this

quiet neck of the woods. Give them their chance, Jassy. Play it up a bit, like you've just been chosen beauty queen, and they'll love you for it."

She moistened her lips nervously and he added quickly: "Heck, there's no problem—not for you. Take it as it comes. They're so open and friendly, so all-fired *easy*, you'll get a real kick out of it."

"Well, thank goodness for that!" She leaned back and felt better.

She liked this man. She liked his broad, humorous face and relaxed informality. She might have known him for five years, not five minutes. Never mind the Surans, she would face them later. The first hurdle was still Ben Lanyard—and Betty Lanyard. She had heard from Mr Chandra that "Mr Ben" had a young sister, "Miss Betty". There was no knowing what her attitude would be.

"Betty was busting her heart to fly to Colombo with us, but Ben wouldn't risk it," said Ray. "She hasn't had all the jabs we've had pumped into us. It's steaming up to the monsoon north of the equator. Smallpox, typhoid, you name it. Bringing an infection back to a small community like this can be a major disaster, so Ben put his foot down."

"I didn't expect it. I was surprised when Mr Chandra suddenly appeared."

"I bet she's sweating it out of Ben right now!" he chuckled. "That's *our* fault! We had to take off twenty minutes early, and had a tail wind most of the way. Well ahead of schedule." He drained his cup and put it on the tray. "I hope you don't mind hanging about like this, but time doesn't seem so mighty important once we've left Sri Lanka—Ceylon, I guess you still call it. When we cross the line we relax."

He picked up the tin of cigarettes, took off the lid, flicked the opener point over with his thumb and pressed the lid firmly on the tin below. The vacuum hissed. He twisted the top round and removed the lid again, taking a thin disc of tinfoil off the cigarettes.

"How often do you 'cross the line'—that's the Equator, isn't it?"

"Regularly every week, unless there's a darn good reason for cancelling a flight. Freight and mail, but not many passengers." He jerked the cigarette tin dextrously and a couple of cigarettes popped up above the level of the rest. Offering her one, he said: "What made you suddenly decide to come out here? It's an awful long way from the high life in London."

"It's even further away from . . . where *you* come from," she countered, veering off the personal question, refusing the cigarette.

"Toronto. You mean you've got cause, and what have *I* got? Well, I'll tell you." He paused, pulling a packet of matches from his pocket and cupping his square hands to shield the flame closely. "No, it's not just another job. I've been around for eight-nine years now. Part of the scenery practically—except to Chan! In his book I'm still a furriner."

"You must like it here very much."

"Yeah," he was quite serious for a moment, "you can sure say that." He drew on his cigarette and blew an expert smoke-ring. "I met Big Ben when he was up at Cambridge. I'd been bumming round the world: hauling freight down in Chile, flying executive jets in California, stunt-flying for film companies, anything I could get. I landed a job in England as an instructor

23

for a flying club. Ben joined the club and our faces seemed to fit." He flicked some ash towards the verandah edge. "We were a couple of hellions!" he added with a reminiscent grin, watching the cigarette ash curl away.

"You came back here with him?"

"No, that was later," he said, serious again. "I guess you know Ben's dad, John Lanyard, was a prisoner of war in Singapore? Well, it pretty near wrecked him. Then your father was killed in a crash. Then his wife died when Betty was born. It got so he couldn't take much more. While Ben was at Cambridge he had a heart attack and Ben had to get back fast."

"What happened?" she asked, her grey eyes intent on him.

"It was okay as far as Bombay. After that Ben was stymied. He couldn't charter a plane—there wouldn't have been anywhere to land anyway. He had to bribe the master of a freighter out of Bombay to make a special run to the islands, but it took longer than he reckoned and he was too late."

"Oh, I'm sorry," she said haltingly, and truly felt it. It was her first contact with the realities of this place, breaking into the dreamlike quality of the whole journey. She hadn't known about John Lanyard; or anything else going on half a world away. She hadn't even thought of asking Uncle Cecil to tell her all *he* knew about the Lanyards, because she had been so absorbed in her own problems. Silly, meaningless problems, focused on Toby Taylor.

"Chan handled everything when John Lanyard died until Ben got back," said Ray. "One of the old school, Chan, and a bit of a stickler, but he's a great guy."

She agreed, nodding eagerly. "But when did you come?"

"Well, Ben was hopping mad about that mess. He wrote me he wasn't going to be thrown by any more emergencies, even if it meant breaking the bank. We had to have an airstrip, aircraft, radio communications—the works. That's Ben: if he set his mind to it he could shift the Pyramids! Every man-jack on the islands worked on the strip one way or another. Took all of three years to get things going."

"And you threw up your job in England to help him out."

"Heck, no!" he retorted, a shade too emphatically. "It was a darn good proposition, laid on the line. Starting a regular service, training the young Surans to take over. It's already breaking even on the special consignments we fly out."

Jassy was fascinated by the glimpse behind the façade. The strip at Sura North Point looked so isolated and bare she had not realised how much time and back-breaking work it must have involved. Her own homecoming would probably not have been arranged without it.

Ray Calver had spent his life in faraway places like this. Looking curiously at him, she said: "Do you ever think about going home—to Toronto, I mean?"

"Sure, I think about it. Some time in the next hundred years, I guess. Everybody needs roots, Jassy. Maybe, if I could've put them down here. . . . Hey!" he protested. "I've unloaded enough. Your turn now."

She drew back instinctively. "There's nothing to tell. . . ."

25

"Casing the joint?" he asked with a grin.

"What a way to put it, Ray!" She couldn't help smiling. "No. Perhaps I'm trying to find my roots too. I've been out of touch with the family all my life, and I was thinking what that meant just now—what you said about John Lanyard and how Ben had to cope."

"Want to know what I think?" He cocked a quizzical eyebrow at her. "I'll lay odds you'll be missing London before you can turn round twice."

She hesitated. "London is a different kind of city for different people," she said slowly, unconscious of the brief shadow in her eyes.

"It was like that, was it?" Stubbing out his cigarette, he questioned bluntly: "Love affair go sour? All right! So tell me to mind my own business."

"Mind your own business," she repeated, tilting her chin.

He threw up his head, laughing. "Lanyard, by golly! Right out of the same mould. Wait till you meet Ben."

"I *am* waiting." His good humour was so infectious that she heaved an exaggerated sigh and said: "And waiting . . . and waiting. . . ."

"Poor old Ben! What with Betty and May-lee, and now you."

"Who's May-lee? Mr Chandra mentioned the name."

"You don't know about May-lee? Oh, brother!" his eyes were still full of laughter. "I think I'm going to enjoy being around for a while."

"Please, Ray—who's May-lee?"

But something had made him turn, looking out across the airstrip. The air was suddenly heavy and the light seemed to alter so swiftly that the brilliance of white, blue and green had gone dark. The patches of sunshine and shadow on the verandah melted together. Beyond the hangar the screen of manioc thickets had become a black wall against the sea. Inland the thick crowns of the palm grove hung motionless.

"Here it comes," said Ray Calver. "Up you get."

Jassy jumped to her feet, rather startled, standing to one side while he moved the table and pushed their chairs back towards the verandah wall. She could see the Surans scrambling into the plane.

Over the palm trees a belt of cloud appeared, moving rapidly across the sky, swelling and rolling in changing shapes as if the mass of billows were alive. In another few seconds the palms were heeling over again. A door in the control block banged as the wind came whipping through the verandah and set the loofah-vine dancing on the picket fence.

Sitting down gingerly on the edge of her chair, Jassy smelt the tang in the wind and watched a dense curtain of rain spreading over the airstrip. It was so heavy that it rose from the ground like mist, beating along the edge of the verandah in a hosing spray.

"Did you think you could leave your umbrella behind in London?" Ray's voice lifted cheerfully above the rattle of the rain. "I guess they'll soon fix you up with one of those plastic rain-capes from the village stores."

If the cargo had been unloaded on to the tarmac, thought Jassy, it would have been well and truly soaked. Including my cases!

Hot dazzling sunshine, then drenching rain and air

as salty as the ocean. "Ray, how can you tell?" she asked, "about the rain?"

"Sometimes you can see the showers coming. Sometimes you just feel 'em. Chan's the expert. He can read the sky like a book."

The downpour thinned and blew away as suddenly as it appeared. A wedge of blue opened over the palm grove, widening as the belt of cloud rolled out to sea. Once it had gone the airstrip lay shimmering in a clear new light and rainwater trickled off the plane in diamond points.

Ray Calver went to the edge of the verandah to lean on the rail. He had his back to her, his broad brown shoulders outlined under the thin nylon shirt. There was something about him, open and dependable —and undemanding. He made things so much easier.

She found herself wondering what he did in Sura between flights, how much time he had to spend away in Colombo—and whether he ever visited Heena.

He was leaning further forward now as if he was listening and watching the road where it disappeared into the palm trees. Her eyes followed his, but there was nothing to be seen. Then after a few moments she caught the sound, like a faint, buzzing throb in the distance. As if to confirm there was something there the Surans were out on the tarmac facing the same way.

Jassy folded her hands tightly in her lap, unconsciously assuming that air of quiet detachment she had long ago learnt to use to mask her feelings. Was it a car? No, heavier; much heavier; more than one engine. A royal convoy, of course! Nothing less for the master of the islands, she thought.

Where was Mr Chandra? He must have heard it too, up in the control room. If Ray went out to the tarmac when they arrived—if he deserted her now—she would need Mr Chandra's reassuring presence to bridge the awkward introductions.

Ray glanced at his watch, straightened up and stretched lazily. "There rides the posse to the rescue. Brace yourself, Jassy."

The first to come bowling down the road out of the tree-line was an old army truck. A little way behind she saw a lorry rather like a small tanker. Last in the convoy was a jeep, its low canvas hood hiding the occupants, its bodywork painted a brilliant yellow shining in the sun.

CHAPTER TWO

JASSY could never quite remember afterwards just what happened in the next few hours. If time had been standing still for a while it suddenly went into a bewildering spin when Ben Lanyard arrived.

The truck bumped off the road across the airfield, circled in an erratic loop and backed up to the plane in a series of jerks with the engine roaring and coughing exuberantly. Down came the tailboard with a bang. A couple of men, a woman and a child clambered out on to the tarmac. There was a buzz of talk, a snatch of laughter on the breeze. They kept turning, looking eagerly towards the control block.

Meanwhile the refuelling bowser, as stately as a small beetle, rolled past the verandah and pulled up by the hangar. The yellow jeep, much further behind than had appeared from a distance, spurted forward and swung round to the control block, peppering the picket fence with loose coral like a shower of grapeshot. The brakes were slammed on to a dead halt and tiny pools of rainwater shuddered with light in the hollows of the canvas hood.

Jassy couldn't see the driver of the jeep, but from the near side a girl jumped out, as slight as a pixie. She wore dark blue slacks and a round-necked, embroidered mandarin jacket of sapphire blue. It looked as though her feet were bare. Her soft, dark brown hair was scooped up into a knot on top of her head with a long, glossy pony-tail.

"Chan-n-n!" her voice rang clear as a bell. "Ra-a-y? Did she come? Where is she? *What's she like*?"

Jassy got to her feet uncertainly.

Ray said, over his shoulder: "That's my gal!" casting up his eyes in mock despair. "Hey, you!" he called. "We're on the verandah."

The girl came up the path in a whirl of eagerness, the soles of her Indian slippers, strung on two loops across the toes, slapping on the soles of her bare feet. Up the plinth of the verandah, pausing for a long moment, she stared at Jassy with her mouth open in a soundless "O-o-o-oh", and then suddenly flung her arms round her in a tight hug. Before Jassy could get her breath, she stood back at arm's length and frankly inspected her from head to foot, blue eyes sparkling and head tilted on one side.

She was impertinent and charming and quite irresistible. Her face was golden brown, a pert oval dusted with darker freckles. Her arms were as speckled as a thrush, and her skin glowed pink under the tan. At first glance she looked about twelve, but there was a roundness and awareness about her figure that was at least five years older.

"Phe-e-ew!" she released a gusty breath. "Ray, will you take a look at that? Doesn't she look super?"

"Super," he agreed promptly, highly amused by the encounter and not least by Jassy's blank astonishment. "Hey now," he said, "hold it a minute! Let's do this right! Jassy, I'd like you to meet Betty Lanyard—as if you hadn't guessed."

The pony-tail swung over. "Idiot," she told him

31

lovingly. "This is *family*."

Family...the very sound of the word gave a sudden lift to Jassy's heart. At the same time she sensed the special relationship between Betty and Ray; the familiarity of affection. Something more than friendship, but not at all self-conscious. Ray had been here so long he must have known Betty since she was a child. He adored her and had probably spent years spoiling her. Jassy could read it in his eyes.

Betty tucked her arm into Jassy's with unaffected glee, off on another tangent.

"Oh, Jassy, you're going to knock Sophena's eye out! Can I call you Jassy? Of course, you don't know Sophena yet. She's Dr Ducase's daughter. You'll be meeting her soon. She thinks she's the only civilised female for ten thousand miles around. Golly," she added bluntly, "if you'd turned out to be some kind of Chelsea freak after all, I'd have died!"

After all?—thought Jassy dazedly—*some kind of Chelsea freak*? It was not in the least offensive, it was funny, like listening to the unguarded chatter of a child.

"You mind your manners," Ray interrupted severely. "The poor girl's only just arrived and you're smothering her with talk already. You haven't let her get a word in edgeways. Not one single word."

"Haven't I? Oh, well! Go on, Jassy...."

There was a brief, disconcerting silence. Ray was grinning. Betty managed to look contrite and impish at the same time. Jassy found herself dissolving into laughter, all her carefully composed reserve gone. After the loneliness and uncertainty, Betty was such a relief.

"I've been wondering about you too," she admitted. "I didn't know what to expect when I got here."

"What's the verdict?" Betty demanded, twirling round on her toes and striking an exaggerated pose like a model in a fashion advertisement.

"*Super!*" Jassy mimicked, her spirits rising into the same bantering mood. "Ray, doesn't she look super?"

They were all laughing now.

Betty said delightedly: "Oh, Jassy London Lanyard!—I'm so glad you've come! Did Ray tell you I wanted to go to Colombo to fetch you? They wouldn't let me—Ben and Ray and Chan and Dr Ducase. Men! They're always ganging up on me, but now you're here you can take my side. May-lee's no good at all. All she can think of saying is 'you do as Ben says'. If he told me to jump off the turtle pen into the lagoon, she'd say 'You just do as Ben says'...

Ben Lanyard ... Jassy had been so taken up with Betty's unconventional, warm-hearted welcome, she had forgotten about Ben.

Her glance flew out to the picket fence. All she could see was the height and breadth of his back dominating the little yellow jeep—it was impossible that he should have come out of such a small space! No wonder Ray had referred to him as "Big Ben". A wryly appropriate kind of joke by the look of it. She also remembered Ray saying "poor old Ben"— poor *old* Ben?

He was standing by the front wheel on the far side, facing away, with a dark green, wide-brimmed, rather battered jungle hat on the back of his head. Underlying Betty's chatter she caught the deep tones of his voice from the distance speaking to the Suran pilot and the postmaster who were walking towards the jeep. Behind them the Surans from the lorry and the men from the airstrip trailed over the tarmac carrying coloured bundles.

Why hadn't Ben Lanyard come over to the verandah first to greet her? He was supposed to be her host, wasn't he? As the disquieting thought welled up she knew Betty had answered it already. Visitor or not, she was family—of a sort. An interruption in the settled routine of his life, to be tolerated because of her name. *Because he had no option*, her conscience told her uncomfortably. *Well, that puts me in my place for a start.*

"I can usually wheedle Chan into persuading Ben, if I try hard enough," Betty was saying, "but Ben wouldn't budge, and Chan wouldn't go against Ben if his life depended on it! All I wanted was a joy-ride, and to meet you, and . . . well . . ." she confessed wistfully, "maybe look round the shops in Colombo for something special to wear for my birthday party. Where's Chan, by the way? I suppose he's gone up to the wireless room?"

Jassy tried to focus her attention. "Your—your birthday? When's your birthday?"

"On the eighteenth of next month, I'll be eighteen!"

"Oh, Betty, I wish I'd known before I left London. If I could have had your size and colour, and so on, I could have brought you something myself. I wish I'd known."

"I thought of that too, but Ben wouldn't . . . I mean, Chan offered to look for something nice for me in Colombo or Bombay," she finished hastily.

Chan again, Jassy reflected dryly. The kindly, reliable, ubiquitous Mr Chandra—instead of the interloper from London. *I wish I'd known more about them all before I plunged into this.* It all seemed a bit petty, but she supposed she would have to put up with Ben's cranky disapproval after the complicated business of getting here. For a few weeks anyway. After all, she had made three allies already, Mr Chandra, Ray, and Betty herself. She would like to stay till Betty's birthday, if Ben didn't make it too difficult.

She threw another look towards the man by the jeep. Then she met Ray's eye for an instant and bit her lip. Almost as if he'd read her mind he said: "Ben's a law unto himself." He sounded momentarily embarrassed. "He's getting things organised. He'll be over in a minute."

Betty turned to Ray, pulled a face at him. She swung back to Jassy, the imp of mischief in her smile again. "Everything's been such a scramble! Ben had to go to Venda with Jimmy this morning because the generator broke down, and he was back very late. May-lee took the message on the two-way telling us you were touching down early. She went into a terrible flap, as usual. Ben had to put up with it all through tiffin. Well, thank heavens I missed that. I came over to Main Bay this morning to give them a hand." She broke off, pointing to the cups. "You've had tea!" she said accusingly.

"What else?" Ray said. "We had to pass the time till the laggards got here."

"Oh, Jassy, they've laid everything on at the Bay already. You *will* try, won't you? I mean, pretend you're longing for tea, and enjoy it all. They've taken so much trouble. You know? It's important. . . ."

Her voice dropped away as she looked at Jassy enquiringly.

"Don't worry, Betty, I won't let you down!"

Jassy smiled with more assurance than she felt. It was rather like telling a child that a party would go well, but she knew that Betty's concern about those others at Main Bay went deeper than that. *Noblesse oblige*?

The voice from the road seemed nearer now; she could hear the words. Ben Lanyard had turned his head. Her palms became clammy, her mouth went dry.

"They're on the verandah," Ben said. "Get the small A-2 crate put on last, nearest the tailboard, Ramu. And her cases, of course. Tao? You'll see to that?" He moved round the jeep, the Surans following him. "How are you going back, Elahi?"

The postmaster's reply was inaudible.

"No, you'd better come back with us. Shove your bike on the truck and sit up front with Bunsi."

They seemed to cluster and follow him to the pathway, like a magnet drawing pins. In another brief glance Jassy saw that the coloured bundles were flowers. For me, she thought, her heart quickly warming; flowers for me!

The deep voice said: "Right, let's get it over with."

"Oh, do hurry up, Ben!" Betty called out, leaning over the verandah rail.

He started up the path and then stopped for a moment, half turned, pulling off the battered hat and spinning it dexterously into the back of the jeep. He had dark hair. His light drill slacks were tucked into calf-length boots, and he wore a zipped bush-jacket of the same colour, open at the neck, with the broad starched cuffs turned back on his brown arms.

He covered the coral in easy strides to the verandah saying: "How did it go, Ray?"

"Okay, commander," said Ray with a mock salute, standing aside for him.

He took the top step and stood stock still, staring at Jassy as Betty had done.

Jassy gazed back at Ben with a faint sense of shock, he was so unlike the mental picture she had conjured up of a middle-aged colonial planter, hearty, red-veined, a bit pompous and rather set in his ways after living too long in the tropics. The first inconsequential thought that popped into her head was: *Oh, heavens!* . . . the Lord High Executioner!

The impression sprang out of his hard brown face under a thatch of crisp dark hair, the deep blue-black eyes and the tight line of his jaw muscles; most of all from the menacing stance as he confronted her on the verandah for the first time, his booted feet planted apart and his sinewy, sunburnt hands on his hips. He had an electrifying aura of authority that owed as much to a tense, leashed energy as to his big physique.

The penetrating directness of his look shattered her a little, but she willed herself not to lower her eyes. She felt acutely shy; and a little bit frightened for no reason at all. She thought: he's too strong, too cocksure . . . he's—he's dangerous. . . .

Their effect on each other seemed to be mutual, as if Jassy was not quite what he had expected either. She had been instantly aware of a fleeting expression suddenly hooded by the surprise in his face. A flick of antagonism or contempt? Distinctly unpleasant, disappearing before she could take it in. Something wordless was happening between them; she did not understand it, but under his long, critical appraisal the colour surged into her cheeks and then drained away leaving her skin pale and luminous. She felt defenceless. In another moment the shutters were down and her bleak mask of detachment was back in place again.

"Good God!" Ben said forcefully.

"D'you get it too, Ben?" Betty bounced off the verandah rail. "The minute I saw her I thought I'd met her before. Then I thought, that's crazy. It must be a kind of family thing."

Jassy, locked tight inside her iciest shell, put her head up and took a pace towards him, holding out her hand.

"I'm glad to meet you at last. How do you do," she said with a chilly politeness that would have done Aunt Dora credit.

Ben closed the gap with a stride. Her barbed formality seemed to have gone right over his head. Instead of shaking her outstretched hand, he grasped her by the arm, turning her into the sunlight and tilting her face up with a finger under her chin.

Jassy was so startled she held her breath for a few seconds. It came to her with a flash of panic that he was going to kiss her, but the deep-set blue-black eyes were inspecting her features with such insolent confidence that she stiffened and stared him out in stony silence.

"Uncanny," he said briskly. "She's the living image

of her grandmother—give or take about fifty years."

Some instinct told her that there was more to his surprise, the blunt inspection she was being subjected to, than her resemblance to her unknown grandmother, however striking it might be; and from Betty's dancing eyes and Ray's knowing grin in the background, they were conscious of it too. There was some joke going on that she could not share. The story of her life had been the jokes she had not been able to share—the sense of separateness, of not belonging. . . . *Not here,* her heart cried, *surely not here too?*

She jerked free, pushing back her hair and rubbing her forehead with her fingertips in a confused gesture. Did Ben Lanyard always behave in this intolerably high-handed way? As though she were an object, not even entitled to the simplest courtesy like a handshake or a brief "hello"! She slowly clenched her hands because she was beginning to tremble with resentment.

"What's the matter, Jassy?" Betty's ingenuous voice sounded anxious now. "You're looking so stand-offish all of a sudden. . . ."

Before she could find an answer, the deep voice interposed : "The fact is that you and I are a couple of backwoods barbarians, Bet." He picked up Jassy's hand, swiftly noting and opening the clenched fingers, and held it for a moment between his hard palms. "How do you do, Jacynth—or dare I call you Jassy after all that?"

"Jassy will do, Mr Lanyard," she said coldly.

"Ben will do, Miss Lanyard," he returned. Jassy looked up sharply, suspecting sarcasm, but saw a glint of wry humour instead. "We have no manners, Jassy, and we've kept you waiting around here long enough.

39

I apologise."

He turned to the Surans clustered by the edge of the verandah, a small group of olive, brown and copper-skinned islanders smiling expectantly at them, waiting for their turn to be introduced to Jassy. Ben seemed to have dismissed the whole uncomfortable episode, just like that, by turning away.

Ray said: "Guess I'll drift off and collect my gear."

Ben beckoned to a man standing near the verandah step and he came forward eagerly, leading a woman who held a little girl of about two years old straddled on her hip.

Both wore sarongs, the man's a dark pattern of gold and green knotted at the waist, with a neat linen jacket buttoned up to the throat, the woman's a gaudy floral cotton wrapped high under the breast, with a short "choli"-style bodice of white muslin. They had loops of flowers hanging from the crooks of their arms. Jassy waited, a little stiff with shyness and constraint.

"These are your people, Jassy—Tao and his wife, Ana. And this," said Ben, gently pinching the child's chin, "is Eta."

My people?... Jassy could not pretend to understand. But she remembered Ray's advice: "It's a great day for them. Give them a chance, Jassy."

"How nice to meet you!" She flashed them the quick, deep smile that transformed her face. She was aware, briefly, that Ben was still watching her.

"There will be much blessings on our house now, Miss Jassy," Tao replied, his sloping eyes vanishing into the creases of his beaming round features as he hung his garland of flowers around Jassy's neck.

He took her hand in both his and touched it lightly to his chest. Ana set the little girl down and clasped hands in the same way. Her garland went on top of Tao's and the flowers were thick about Jassy's face and drenched with the scent of jasmine.

"Eta, see who has come," said Ana, propelling the child towards Jassy.

"Hello, Eta." Jassy stooped into the swinging loops of blossom, ruffling the silky coal-black hair, all her shyness gone as she charmed the child. "What a big girl you are!"

"And the prettiest ever, aren't you, pet?" said Betty.

"And the most naughty, I tell you true, Miss Jassy," Ana informed her.

Ana was beautiful, Jassy thought, with her high cheekbones and sloe eyes, and her hair coiled in a smooth black coronet on top of her head.

Ana was also practical, and very conscious of her privileged position. As Jassy straightened she carefully eased the garlands at the back, lifted Jassy's hair and patted it into position over the flowers on her neck. Then she took immediate possession of the floppy straw hat and carry-bag from the wicker chair and stationed herself like a willowy lady-in-waiting at Jassy's elbow.

To Jassy's surprise it was Tao who made the rest of the introductions and not Ben Lanyard, and when she looked round surreptitiously for the tall figure she saw that he had gone after Ray, was talking to him by the jeep. In a way it was a relief not to have him there; not to have those critical dark eyes taking in every move she made.

The small verandah was soon crowded and she

scarcely had time to think—let alone worry about what Ben Lanyard might be thinking. What did it matter what he thought, anyway? Everyone else seemed to be delighted she had come; overwhelmed, in fact. They pressed forward, their faces shining with welcoming smiles. Tao was in his element shepherding them about her in some kind of unspoken order of precedence and putting unfamiliar names to their bright, animated faces. She met the Suran pilot, Ramu, and the workers from the strip who had sat so patiently by the plane. Elahi, the postmaster, insisted on a second, formal introduction, winking broadly at her and presenting her with a little bunch of marigolds obviously picked from the clumps near the control block. Bunsi, the truck driver, told her exuberantly, without a trace of self-consciousness, that he was a master-mechanic and that none of them would have been there to meet her so quickly without his skill in fixing the generator on Venda in double-quick time that morning.

Jassy, thawing out like an iceberg in the sunshine of their uninhibited cheerfulness, was swept along on a tide of elation and self-confidence. They heaped more garlands of marigolds, jasmine and clove-scented dianthus over her head. She smiled a great deal, answered questions, shook their hands. Over the hub-bub of voices she heard the clatter of Billy clearing the tea cups.

Almost as soon as it had begun it was over, and Tao was leading the exodus back to the plane, urging the men to get the truck loaded as soon as possible and not keep Miss Jassy waiting any more. Ana came and removed the additional garlands and posies with a proprietorial air. Jassy, her face pink with effort, her eyes alight, was still a little dazed by the warmth of real pleasure that had surrounded her. They had all been so genuinely happy to see her that in spite of Ben's behaviour this strange homecoming had begun to mean something.

The verandah seemed very quiet and deserted all of a sudden, with just Jassy, Betty, Ana and the child Eta. Jassy realised that there had been no one called May-lee among the introductions, but as she turned to ask Betty about it Mr Chandra came out of the control building.

Betty flung herself at him. "Chan! You crafty old thing! You've been hiding upstairs."

"Such a thing to say," he protested mildly, allowing himself to be pushed into a chair. "Why you were not here to meet us, eh?"

"That wasn't our fault. Tell him what a rush we had, Ana."

Ana smiled. "No matter now."

She pulled up another chair, installed Jassy in it, and busied herself sorting the posies and garlands on the table into a more convenient arrangement to carry. Jassy was rather embarrassed by the way Ana had taken her over.

Eta tried to climb on Mr Chandra's knee, but Betty swung her up into her arms instead, straddling the child easily on her hip as Ana had done.

"Did you get me something in Bombay, Chan? You said you would look."

"What would an old man know of finery for young ladies?"

Even Jassy could see the quiet twinkle, and it was not lost on Betty.

"You did manage it? What? A dress length?"

He shook his head solemnly.

"Oh, Chan, you are infuriating!"

"Very well," he relented. "I have brought you a sari. Real silk, with silver embroidery. You will see."

"You're an angel!" She lifted Eta high in the air, planted a resounding kiss on the child's cheek and set her down again. "Is it still on the plane, Chan? I could go and fetch it."

"No, childee. Better if Tao takes it with Miss Jassy's things for Heena."

"I must speak with Tao. I will tell him," said Ana. She finished bundling the flowers and put Jassy's hat and carry-bag neatly beside them on a chair. The child trotted towards her but she patted her away. "Eta, you stay Miss Jassy. You be good, Eta."

"The parcel, Ana. On the rack in the cabin with Mr Ray's case. Tell Tao he would not crush it, eh?"

Ana left the verandah for the strip where Tao could be seen above the tailboard of the truck and Ramu at the loading hatch of the plane, with all the other men lending a hand between them, heaving and shouting in concert as the cargo was hoisted from one to the other.

Staring uncertainly after her mother at first, Eta decided to accept her departure and became absorbed in the possibilities of Jassy's carry-bag which lay temptingly within reach if she stood at full stretch on tiptoes.

The sun slanted under the roof of the verandah, panelling it with light, so warm that Jassy felt the weight of the garlands clinging around her neck like a heavily scented scarf.

44

One more stop at Main Bay, and then Heena—in spite of the heat she was savouring her success. By some mysterious means, within the last few minutes she had discovered a way with the Surans, and it was not just the novelty and excitement that had carried her along but a spontaneous response to them on her part. Her shyness had completely disappeared as some deeper feeling, almost instinct, had taken over.

She could hold her own now. Except where Ben Lanyard was concerned.

Meeting Ben had only confirmed her wariness of him. Ray's informality had put her at her ease; Betty's was childlike and endearing. Ben's was different. His lack of ceremony came from a blunt, assertive confidence in his right to say and do as he pleased. She suspected that she would soon be taking orders too if she allowed it, and she had no intention of falling meekly into line with the rest of the dependants! Something bumped into her legs and she looked down, startled, at Eta's downy black head. She picked the child up and cuddled and tickled her till they were both giggling unrestrainedly.

Ben had been putting down the hood of the yellow jeep, and as he returned to the verandah Mr Chandra rose at once to meet him.

Ben gripped his arm. "Well, old friend? Ray's been telling me. Thank you for handling everything so smoothly."

"It was my privilege, Mr Ben."

"I hope the heat didn't knock you up too much."

"No, no! The humidity is trying, of course, Bombay especially. I was more worried for Miss Jassy, but as you see there is no harm. The cases for Eastern

45

Trading will go air-freight to San Francisco tomorrow. I have personally arranged it."

"Good. Did you get the cargo schedules?"

"All settled. And a tanker from Abadan in two weeks."

"Right. I'll be on Miro tomorrow morning, but we can go through the rest after tiffin. Take it easy till tomorrow afternoon, understood? No more now."

He seemed impatient to leave and he and Mr Chandra went back to the jeep, still chatting. Ana came up the steps smiling, picked up Jassy's things and, much to Jassy's amusement, instead of taking the child from her she carefully arranged the straw cart-wheel of a hat on Jassy's head. Ana considered the result and then as if satisfied said: "Come, we go now, Miss Jassy."

Down the pathway the sun began to draw the scent of the flowers, particularly where they were crushed against Eta's warm little body, making it feel rather like walking through a fragrant hothouse. Betty linked her arm on the other side, squeezing it now and then as she bubbled with enthusiasm. The coral under Jassy's sandals, the gourds rattling in the loofah vine, the fringe of swaying palm trees, even the sound of the ocean pounding on the reef beyond the manioc thickets appeared different somehow.

"Who's sharing my lap?" Ray asked with a grin as they reached the jeep.

Ben said briskly: "Jassy in front with me, Mr Chandra and Ana at the back. You and Betty can hop a ride on the sides."

He took the child from Jassy and helped her into the front seat while Ray manoeuvred Ana and Mr

Chandra into the little vehicle. Eta gave the big, sun-burnt man a beguiling smile, bumping up and down in his arm until he tweaked her nose very gently with a chuckle and plumped her back on to Jassy's lap as a matter of course. From under her lashes Jassy watched and wondered at the softened expression on that hard brown face.

As he slid his long length behind the wheel he turned to make sure Ray had found Betty a safe position. "All set," Ray told him, "I'll keep an eye on her."

Ben lifted an arm and the truck roared to life on the tarmac and set out ahead of them across the air-strip to the road. Then the jeep rolled forward, coral rubble crackling like pistol shots under the wheels and the good wishes of the airstrip workers ringing around Jassy's head as they gathered speed.

Jassy caught a glimpse of the shining water of the lagoon before the road curved inland towards the line of palm trees. The nearer they came the higher they seemed to soar—sixty, eighty, some perhaps even a hundred feet high—running along the perimeter of the clearing like a row of sentinels. They passed through the line and Jassy sat up, staring around in amazement.

What she had thought of as a grove was a vast plantation stretching away on every side; palms by the thousand, evenly ranged along grassy aisles, their tall, bare trunks bowing to the wind and spilling over at the top in fountains of leaves. Jassy could never have imagined a forest as spacious, strange and beautiful as this, spanning out in endless vistas of colonnades and avenues.

Across the aisles, among the thicker, ringed trunks

and tattered crowns of the mature palms, slender, tufty young ones had been planted out in regular sequence to regenerate the whole plantation. The old trunks bulged out at the bottom, gripping the earth as they leaned over, and some of them had been painted white about a foot up from the base as if they were markers of some kind. The long shafts creaked and swayed and the great green leaves clattered overhead.

Jassy craned her head back to gaze up at the crests. Line after line, she found heavy crops hanging under the leaves, at every growing stage from smooth green ovals to thick dark clusters, and here and there an enormous nut suddenly dropped with a thud in the pull of the wind from the sea.

As the jeep raced along the white coral surface cutting a highway through the avenues, zebra bars of sunlight and shadow from the trees flickered rhythmically up and down. Sometimes a lone seabird took flight, or a flock of indignant sparrows fluttered away, startled by the movement.

Ben drove at speed, his sunburnt hands resting lightly on the wheel, his eye on the road, but he was aware of the stir of interest beside him and eased off on the accelerator to give Jassy time to take it in.

"*Cocos nucifera*," he said. "A big part of our business."

"Coconuts?" All her reserve and formality vanished in her eagerness to know more. "I had no idea it would be like this! How many are there, Ben? . . . the trees, I mean."

"In these stands, about forty-five thousand. We have another plantation on St George, across the lagoon, and a couple of thousand acres on the offshore islands.

48

And the nurseries—plenty of good young stock in the nursery stands."

"All with coconuts!"

He seemed amused. "Around eighty nuts from each in one crop. Up to a hundred on the mature palms."

"That must run into . . . *millions*!"

"Millions," he agreed dryly.

"How on earth do you get at them all?"

"I'll take you round and show you one of these days," he swung the wheel over to take the curve of the road where another highway of white coral branched off through the coconut plantation, "if you're here long enough."

"If I'm here?" The implication sank in. Something inside her tightened into a spurt of unaccustomed anger. "Are you already planning to send me back to England on the next flight out?" she asked, biting her lip.

He shot a quick glance at her: so town-bred and elegant in a pink summer dress with light thonged fashion sandals on her long slender feet. Two swathes of walnut-gold hair framed her pale patrician face, and her grey eyes were narrowed against the glare, giving an appearance of cold disdain.

"I'm sure you'll be bored to tears in a few days," was his brusque comment.

"That's a pretty sweeping assumption to make the minute I've got here. I can't see how you could possibly know," she answered tonelessly. "Do you particularly pride yourself in being able to make spot judgements?"

Without waiting for a reply she half-turned her head. "Would you pass me my dark glasses, please,

49

Ana? They're somewhere at the top of my bag." She reached behind to take them. "Thanks."

As she slid them on to her nose the cool greyness of the lenses not only cut off the harsh sunlight but gave her a flimsy sense of security, putting an imaginary barrier between herself and this boorish, infuriating man who, within the short space of an hour, had succeeded in making her feel uncomfortable, unwelcome, inadequate and resentful. And now angry . . . so unreasonably angry, when all she wanted was to relax and enjoy all the new experiences and be happy the way she felt with everyone else.

"Hoity-toity!" the deep voice said softly, almost scathingly.

Secure behind the big, dramatic frames of the dark glasses, she stared at his profile. She was lost this time, even for a perfunctory retort. No matter what Uncle Cecil had said this was her *host*—this hostile creature! How was she going to cope with Ben Lanyard? She couldn't avoid him, here on his own home ground, but she would have to shut herself away again as she had been shutting herself away all her life, from people who could provoke her feelings, and from the rebuffs that hurt so much.

CHAPTER THREE

IN another few moments the open acres of the palm
forest were left behind and the road plunged into a
dense green woodland of towering trees. The crusty
trunks were covered with thick foliage and looped
with mossy lianas, and in between, crowding every
inch of fertile land, were clumps of wild palms tangled
with flowering creepers. Sleek black mynah birds
fluttered away at the sound of the truck, vanishing
into the luxuriant undergrowth. Jassy suddenly realised
what overwhelming labour it must have involved to
keep the plantation clear and carve an airstrip out of
a wilderness like this.

After a while the trees thinned out again, although
a mass of shrubs still flooded down each side of the
road like a green tide as the jeep coasted down towards
Main Bay.

Unlike his French contemporaries who held the
possession en jouissance of other oil islands of the
Indian Ocean but preferred to live in France or
Mauritius, the old English sea-captain, Harry Lanyard,
had made the Suran Islands his own, and the encamp-
ment of wooden huts built by his early colonists at
Sura Main Bay had spread slowly inland along
wandering lanes as Arab, Malay and Indian seafarers
had asked to be allowed to settle in the sheltering
crescent of Lanyard's atoll. Whatever their origins two
centuries ago, Mr Chandra had told Jassy proudly,

they were all Surans now and lived together without fear or favour.

Driving down one of these winding avenues, shaded by breadfruit trees, Indian almond and cassias, Jassy was enchanted by the cottages built of rough chunks of coral set in mortar, neatly thatched and decorated with patterns of shells set in the walls. Doors and shuttered windows were wide open to the breeze, but to Jassy's disappointment there was not a single islander to be seen.

At the end of the avenue the heart of the village of Main Bay fanned out in front of them, taking Jassy's breath away—a great semi-circle of lawns and flower beds ringed with buildings, and beyond that a scimitar of golden sand melting into miles of shimmering water like liquid glass and the distant forms of other islands crouching in the haze across the lagoon.

Ben braked the jeep in the shade of an enormous, grotesque *peepul* tree. Bunsi, the truck driver, blared a tune on his horn. Materialising as if from nowhere, the people of Main Bay came pouring out from every corner of the village. Jassy sat petrified. She wanted to scramble out and run away; she couldn't even move. Her legs felt like lead and her heart was bumping erratically. Someone—it was Betty—came round and whisked Eta off her lap. She clasped her trembling hands tightly together in an agony of shyness, staring at the crowd that was gathering rapidly, growing every moment before her eyes until there were at least five or six hundred congregated on the green. If she'd known about this . . . if she'd suspected the surprise they had planned . . .

There was no particular national style of dress

among the Surans, only a conglomeration of coloured cottons in shirts and shorts, loose jackets with sarongs, saris with choli bodices, long Muslim pyjamas, short-sleeved shift dresses with patterns of flowers all over them. A group of elderly men and women, more formally clothed, detached themselves and came forward, a smiling reception committee, as Jassy could see, bowing and folding their hands together with old-fashioned courtesy even at that distance.

Ben unfolded his long legs and got out in one sweeping movement, and promptly walked away towards them.

Feeling all at once as appalled as she would have felt if she had been thrust on to the platform of the Albert Hall to face a packed audience alone, Jassy's thoughts reached out to him, willing him to come back. Why had he left her? Why had he deserted her now? Was it just his casual way, his own self-confidence making him insensible to the ordeal it might be for her? Or was he testing her again, holding off to see what sort of impression she would make? She had the others with her—why should it matter whether Ben was with her or not? Incredibly, it mattered.

Then Ray was on one side of her, helping her out of the jeep with a "didn't I warn you?" grin on his face; and Ana was on the other, brushing the creases from her pink dress, smoothing her gold hair over the garlands and being so attentive with such unruffled calm that Jassy began to recover. Ana held the carry-bag for her. The heat and excitement had brought beads of perspiration to her upper lip; she pressed it away with a tissue, touched up her face from a compact, adjusted her hat and drew herself up into a nonchalant attitude that covered the tumult of uncertainty.

"Golly!" said Betty enthusiastically, hitching Eta's weight higher on her arm. "That's a gorgeous dress, Jassy—not a bit crushed!"

That was why she had bought it, with other new clothes for the trip, in the kind of fabric from which creases slipped easily away. When was it?—only last week? It might have been years ago, on some distant planet.

Mr Chandra, who had been hovering discreetly in the background, seemed to think she was in good hands and, nodding encouragingly at her, set off with a slow, stooping walk along the road around the green.

Ray said: "Time you went over and knocked 'em in the aisles, Jassy-gal! D'you want a tip?"

"Anything!"

"When it's over tell Ben, at the top of your voice, that you'd like to ask for a day's school holiday for the kids! It'll work a treat!"

"I'll try and remember. . . ." He was moving away with Betty and Jassy panicked. "Aren't you staying with me?"

"We'll see you later, at the school-house," Betty informed her blithely.

Jassy was turning to approach the crowd on her own when, as if he were throwing her a lifeline, Ben came striding back. His look ranged insolently over her as he said: "You'll do!"

She hated him for the knowing glint in his eye and found herself answering in a suppressed voice: "D-don't you d-dare patronise me, you—you—deserter!"

The dark brows shot up. "Didn't you want me to keep them at bay while you pulled yourself together?"

Perversely she hated him still more for having understood how she was feeling. All she could say helplessly was: "Oh!" She almost stamped her foot ... because he was mocking her again ... and because she needed him.

"They'll want a good look at you," he said gravely, removing her dark glasses and handing them to Ana. "Come on."

He tucked her hand in his arm and when she made a feeble effort to resist interlaced her fingers firmly with his and walked her over to the Surans. Immediately the sense of strain began to evaporate. She met the reception committee first, the elders of the village of Main Bay itself. After that a lane opened in the crowd and hundreds of delighted faces surrounded her.

It was an extraordinary, exhilarating experience. To Jassy, who had often felt completely isolated in an anonymous mass of Londoners each absorbed in their own concerns, the idea that such a large, friendly mob had gathered just to see and greet *her* was unbelievable.

There were representatives from all five islands, which accounted for the barges, pirogues and a variety of small craft bobbing on the incoming tide outside a large barn of a boatyard at the far end of the beach. Ben introduced as many of the islanders as possible; boatmen, fishermen, gangers from the plantations, foremen from the factories, wives, mothers and daughters. There were scores of children too, as perky and curious as brown sparrows. Everyone spoke

English with a distinctive accent and turn of phrase.

The response of the women, particularly the older ones, surprised Jassy most of all. They pressed as close as they could, occasionally stroking her arm, sometimes gently fingering the fabric of her dress, and remarking loudly on her hair, her smooth complexion, and how beautiful she was. As she moved slowly along at Ben's side, as though she were walking in a dream, she was confronted by an old crone, stooping over two sticks, who looked up with her shrivelled face and sharp eyes beaming and said: "You have come to be Mister Ben's lady, no?"

"No," Jassy shook her head hastily, colour flooding her face. "I'm Tom Lan—I'm Mister Tom's daughter."

"You are Mister Ben's woman," the other insisted. "I have heard everywhere. It is good."

Another woman interposed confidingly as she edged the bent figure out of the way: "The old ones are saying you have come as wife for Mister Ben and they are pleased!"

Hot with embarrassment, Jassy flicked a glance at Ben, but to her relief he was talking to one of the men on the other side of him; and his firm voice continued, never raised but used with effortless authority to keep them moving through the crowd until Jassy found that they were back at the gnarled *peepul* tree again. Although she was a bit confused she faced the Surans and said shakily, yet clear enough for all to hear: "Can the children have a day's holiday from school, Ben, just this once, to celebrate?"

"I think we can fix it." He threw up his head laughing as the children went wild. Then quietly, as the crowd began to disperse: "You did well, Jassy."

"I enjoyed it," she told him simply, pulling her hand out of his grasp.

With that flickering expression that suggested he was perplexed about her in some way, he said brusquely: "Over to the school-house now."

One of the many turnings off the green led into a short lane blazing with the yellow glory of allamanda shrubs. A couple of old-fashioned pony-carts stood in the shade of a group of palms, the horses cropping the grass, raising slow, inquisitive heads as Ben ushered Jassy to a broad gap between the shrubs serving as a gate. The school-house materialised as a rectangular building on a high plinth under a vast, thatched roof. There was no door, only a wide arch for an entrance where shadowy figures could be seen against the cool darkness inside.

"Dear child . . . dear child. . . ."

A little cottage loaf of a woman in a dowdy, tightly-belted navy blue dress, with her grey hair scraped back in a loose knot, came out to meet them. Her scrubbed face shone pink as she held out eager arms.

"Dear child!" Her hands closed on Jassy's arms, squeezing gently. "I can hardly believe it, but one only has to look at you to see. . . ." Her voice was suspended.

"She's all yours, Jonesy," said Ben, glinting affection in his eyes. "This is Miss Nora Jones, Jassy. She runs the hospital and plans all our lives for us."

Obeying an impulse she had never felt in her life before, Jassy bent and put a light kiss on the weathered cheek of this complete stranger.

"So like Jassy used to be—I mean your grand-mother, child." Miss Jones' faded blue eyes were brimming. "And Tom, such a fine lad—"

"In a moment she'll be telling you exactly how she brought your father into the world!"

"Oh, you hush, Ben Lanyard," she chuckled weepily. "I saw you into the world too, so you can mind your manners!"

Scowling ferociously at her, he scooped her up in a long arm, and despite her half laughing, half indignant protests carried her over and set her down on the top step of the school-house. The four of them went in laughing.

This time Jassy could face everyone with much more assurance. She had already met most of the twenty or thirty people in the hall, mainly the elders of the village and the consultative council of the islands who had been on the green. Mr Chandra was already there, accompanied now by his daughter and her husband; Betty, flushed with pleasure and excitement, was helping to organise tea, and Ray, leaning lazily against a table in the background, gave Jassy the thumbs-up sign.

Ana said: "Give me hat, Miss Jassy," and relieving her of the hat and the garlands went to join the women setting plates and cups on trays.

Jassy looked around the "school-house" with wide-eyed curiosity. It seemed to consist of a single enormous hall, and the most remarkable feature was the fact that three of the four walls were only about four feet high, filling the space with clear, even light and allowing the cool air to circulate freely. Chairs and desks had been drawn to the sides. Long screens of plaited palm, presumably used to divide up the classes and covered with maps and childish drawings, stood in a neat row at one end, while at the other end a buffet table had been spread with white damask cloths, beautiful Victorian silver and various tea services loaned by the ladies of the village.

There were large earthenware jars of flowers around the hall, and everything had been arranged so painstakingly that Jassy could understand why Betty had been so anxious about her showing her appreciation. Pushing Ben Lanyard firmly to the back of her mind, she shook off the last vestiges of shyness and constraint and set herself out to make friends.

An introduction to "Miss Millie" and "Miss Mary" who ran the school had a touch of awkwardness at first. They were sisters, middle-aged Eurasians with smooth, sallow skins the colour of old silk and clear, modulated voices; very precise, very meticulous in dress, very formal in manners. Jassy thought guiltily about the school holiday.

"I—I hope you'll forgive me," she faltered, as they all accepted cups of tea from a tray Ana was carrying round. "I asked Ben—Mr Lanyard—about a day's holiday for the children and I realise now that I should have consulted you first. I don't know what you must think of me. . . ."

Mollified by her smile, and her hesitant apology, they began to unbend, assuring her that they had heard about it, that they would have had to get Mr Lanyard's permission in any case—and they approved, of course. They persisted in calling her Miss Lanyard —refusing to accept the familiarity of "Jassy"—but when they found that she was genuinely interested in them, they told her a good deal about the management of the school. Each island had its own crêche and primary school, but as soon as they were old enough the children from all the islands attended the school-house, crossing the lagoon to Main Bay for morning or afternoon sessions. The most gifted senior boys and girls were tutored by a Mr Deshwa Das.

"Have I met him?" Jassy enquired thoughtfully, sipping her tea. "I can't seem to remember the name."

"Alas, he's not been well enough today to be here," Miss Millie confided in a significant tone. "He was with Mr John Lanyard and Dr Ducase in a Japanese prisoner-of-war camp, Miss Lanyard, and has never quite recovered. He's confined to a wheel-chair, you know, but he has a truly brilliant mind."

"D.D. was very disappointed." Ben's voice, unexpectedly behind her, made her hand jerk, clattering the cup against the saucer. "He's anxious to see you. I'll arrange it as soon as he's fit enough."

"I'd like that," she asserted with a fixed smile because his manner was peremptory and Miss Millie and Miss Mary had exchanged glances.

Miss Millie said hurriedly, with what sounded like an excuse for Ben: "Mr Lanyard is deeply concerned about Mr Deshwa Das's health. As we all are, of course. But he more than others, I daresay, as Mr Deshwa Das was his own tutor for many years. . . ."

"I would be just as concerned if it were you or Miss Mary," he said.

He was not being polite. He meant what he said; and when Jassy saw the expressions the two women turned to him, she knew she had glimpsed the secret of his authority in the islands. It was not merely the Lanyard heritage, a feudal authority he could exercise by right. And although the imperious male in him would appeal to most of the women, and his forceful character probably dominated most of the men, it was not that either. It was the quite simple fact that, however autocratic he might seem, Ben Lanyard really cared about them all. He was totally committed to their interests—and they knew it.

This brief insight served to ease the unreasoning hostility which had been building up inside Jassy, even when he declared unceremoniously: "I think you ought to circulate." It was an order, but she took it lightly. Clutching her tea-cup, she moved into the adjoining group of people.

"May I introduce Mr Bender and Dr Ducase?"

Mr Bender was the pastor, as his black and white clerical collar proclaimed. As he clasped her hand firmly, stooping his shoulders and bending his head with a curious little gesture, she could see the thin strands of his hair meticulously brushed across the top of his bald patch. He beamed at her over his spectacles, saying how much he had been looking forward to this moment.

The doctor was short and wizened. His shrewd eyes sparkled from a mass of wrinkles under a shock of grey-white hair.

"So! I've been watching and listening to you, young woman. I must say Ben's a lucky young man to have acquired such a modest, radiant addition to the family." Holding her hand away from him, he turned her slightly one way, then the other, noting the soft flush that crept into her cheeks.

"Ah!" he sighed heavily, "if only I were thirty years younger!"

Jassy couldn't resist flirting with the puckish,

benignly humorous little doctor. "Ah!" she responded soulfully, "if only I were *ten* years older!"

He was delighted. "Well, I must say!" The old eyes disappeared in wrinkles of amusement. "So pretty—and so tactful!"

"Have you been abroad much before, Miss Lanyard?" Mr Bender asked.

"Please call me Jassy. No, I haven't, except for a few weeks' holiday on the Continent. This is all very new and exciting for me."

"I'm sure you'll like living on the garden."

"The garden?"—what a strange way to put it, she thought, the whole place was a tropical garden. Did one live in a garden, or on a garden? Lightly she said: "What garden is that?"

"The Garden of Eden," the doctor promptly twinkled at her, "complete with Adam and Eve."

"I mean Heena," Mr Bender explained, smiling benevolently. "I should have remembered you are not yet familiar with our use of terms in the Oil Islands. When we speak of 'the garden' we mean the place where the fresh produce is grown, fruits and vegetables, not a flower-garden. Most of the produce is grown on Heena, and we refer to it as 'the garden' here."

"I'll have to learn quite a lot of things!" Her look strayed to Ben and then hastily away again. He was talking to Mr Chandra, in that characteristic stance, booted feet apart and his thumbs hooked in the pockets of his slacks, but she still had an uncomfortable impression that he was watching and assessing her behaviour.

"Where's my beautiful daughter?" Dr Ducase

demanded. "Have you met yet? You and she can learn together, when you're not gossiping about all the elegant things young ladies talk about in Europe." He raised his bushy head: "Feena?"

"Don't shout, Father dear. I'm here behind you," said a silky voice as the girl moved round to them holding tapering, delicately manicured hands over her ears and shaking her head reproachfully. "I'm Sophena Ducase." She extended her fingertips with a winsome smile. "Is it permitted to call you Jassy?" That hint of an accent—French?—was rather beguiling.

So this was the "Sophena" who apparently considered herself "the only civilised female for ten thousand miles around". Betty's artless remark had probably sprung from a subconscious tinge of envy— a natural enough reaction.

Sophena was a bit taller than her father, but willowy and fragile, with bouffant flaxen hair and long, narrow, almond-green eyes; superbly chic in filmy white organdie over a pale green underslip, with insets of expensive lace down the front of the bodice and around her creamy throat and wrists. She looked so slight and ethereal that Jassy was reminded of one of those dandelion puffballs that would float away in fragments on a breath of air.

"Yes, do call me Jassy." As the doe eyes slid over her and the sleek, impersonal hand touched hers lightly, she drew herself up a little. Somehow this woman made her feel very lanky and gauche, and clumsy with her tea-cup.

"We must be friends," Sophena rippled. "Fellow exiles, *n'est-ce pas*?"

Instinctively Jassy was on her mettle, though she could not have explained why; something in the look they had exchanged perhaps. A cool elusiveness and touch of hauteur, deadened her face and voice. "I don't feel I've been exiled, I've had such a marvellous welcome. Are you here on a visit too, Miss Ducase?"

Sophena's eyes narrowed for an instant, then she gave a dulcet laugh: "You're a Lanyard all right—that much is clear! But please, my name is Sophena. And I've been living in Geneva for many years now."

The doctor intervened. "She's an interpreter," he informed Jassy proudly. He put an arm about Sophena, but she sidled away from creasing her dress. He added, "One of those international organisations with a string of initials!"

"Talk—talk—talk!" Sophena pressed her fingers to her forehead, then threw her hands out in an expressive fluttering motion. "The demands those men made! It became too much for me."

"My little girl's been working too hard. She needs sunshine and rest."

Looking at her Jassy was hard put to believe that such an exquisitely clothed, frail-looking creature had ever had to do a day's real work in her life, and immediately felt ashamed of her own ungenerous reactions.

"Not too much sunshine! *Non!*" Sophena shuddered daintily. "With my delicate skin there is no tan, only burning and redness. So vulgar!"

At this point Betty frisked into the circle offering sandwiches on one plate and small, round pastries on another. "Try one of these, Jassy," she held up the pastries. "Flavoured with sesame seeds. Do you like it?"

Jassy bit into it and savoured the nutty taste. "Delicious!"

Betty turned to proffer the plate to Sophena, but unfortunately brushed her arm. A couple of pastries tilted off, flicking past the immaculate organdie.

"Oh, *Betty*!" the silky voice was suddenly petulant as Sophena shrank back, fingering her dress for imaginary spots and crumbs.

Betty flushed to the roots of her hair. "I'm sorry, Sophena. It was an accident, honestly...." Jassy's heart went out to her in her confusion.

Sophena recovered herself swiftly. Her tone was soft and gently reproving. "Why are you always so awkward, *petite*? *Doucement, doucement*. Go more quietly, like a lady." She patted her hair fastidiously into place.

Betty moved away to serve the others, her head and her colour high.

"Such a hoyden," Sophena confided in a rueful murmur. "She could be so attractive and well-mannered with proper guidance at this difficult age. Me, I have tried since I have been here," she shook her cloudy butter-blonde hair and shrugged. "What can one expect when she spends so much time with that coarse Suran woman, May-lee? Perhaps you can influence her, *chérie*—"

"I wouldn't dream of trying," Jassy cut in with a frigid smile, suddenly angry inside. "Betty's so open and unspoilt. I like her the way she is."

May-lee again . . . damn May-lee!—whoever she is, thought Jassy crossly.

Taken aback at her icy manner, Sophena was silent

for a moment, almond eyes veiled by faintly tinted, drooping lids. Her laugh, when it came, had sharpened a little. "The family closes up against outsiders, I see. Betty has a certain charm, but unspoilt she is not! Ben indulges her all the time."

"What am I being accused of?" as Ben joined them she lifted a melting gaze up to him. "You look beautiful today, Sophena. I could indulge *you* all the time."

"*Merci*, Monsieur Lanyard!" she returned smoothly. All her attention was now given to Ben. "I may just take you up on that one of these days."

Jassy's eyes flew to his face but could make nothing of the enigmatic look on it. Sophena's was easier to read, a trifle coy, but very appealing, and there was no mistaking that sparking awareness between them.

The party soon began to break up, as if Ben had given some kind of signal. Jassy was busy shaking hands and thanking people when Jimmy Renton invited them over to the guest-house for a drink before they left for Heena. He was Ben's assistant, manager of the factories, a capable, rather florid young man who had talked a great deal about himself and his experiences in the Seychelles and the Chagos Archipelago before coming to Lanyard Estates.

Jassy didn't care for his bold eyes and the too long clasp of his slightly sweaty hand, but she would have liked a glimpse of the old Lanyard house which her father must have known and loved. There was no time to waver because Ben refused the invitation with blunt finality, and the smile faded from Jassy's face as she realised how loath she was to leave this pleasant little oasis for yet another ordeal of strangeness at Heena.

Ray, who had been helping Betty and the two schoolmistresses to rearrange the hall, came across to her, winking broadly. She turned to him eagerly, as to an old friend.

"You did fine!" he said bracingly, under his breath.

"Ray, you should have told me to ask Miss Millie and Miss Mary first about the school holiday. It was a bit sticky, breaking the ice!"

"So I should. But you've got to admit it was a sensation out there with the kids, Jassy-gal. Right?" He flicked her cheek with a light finger.

"Right." She was smiling again, up into his face, curiously reassured.

His glance went beyond her, over her shoulder. He grinned, his eyes wary for a fleeting second. "What's bugging you, Commander? Don't you approve of the V.I.P. consorting with the hired help?"

"Like hell I do," Ben said equably, but Jassy sensed his taut displeasure. "I'll take Jassy down to the beach now, Ray. Round up that officious scamp of ours, there's a good chap."

"Sure," Ray agreed cheerfully, and went off to find Betty.

"Will he be coming with us?" Jassy clutched hopefully at a straw.

"Where?"

"To Heena," she said stiffly, irritated by the arrogant tone.

"Why should he?" was the terse answer. "Ray lives at the guest-house."

Tao and Ana were waiting on the steps of the school-house as they emerged, Tao carrying Eta fast asleep in his arms. Miss Jones and the doctor joined them.

It was a magnificent evening. Sunset hung behind the trees on the rise, seaward of Sura, blazing the sky with colour and throwing long, deep shadows in the village. Looking upwards, Jassy gasped at the canopy of indigo-blue shot with streamers of saffron in a brief tropical brilliance. The clouds were riding high, feathering away into faint, smoky trails of light. The lagoon had become as dark as wine, and the other islands had vanished in a pale, milky vapour along the eastern horizon.

The air was like balm, full of the lingering scents of flowering shrubs and the earthy smell of trodden grass. There were still a few boats in the bay, one or two pirogues already beached on the sands; and there were still a few people out on the green, sitting under the *peepul* tree, strolling along the waterside, their voices fluctuating on a light breeze.

This time Jassy crossed the green between Miss Jones and the little doctor, who had decided to come and see them leave, keeping her distance for as long as possible from the irrational animosity which seemed to keep flaring up between Ben Lanyard and herself. She had been so bemused by the sight of the crowd when she arrived that she had scarcely taken in the extent of the buildings round the green. Apart from the school, a small white church and cottages set in garden plots, Main Bay was a small port. Jonesy and the doctor pointed out each group of square, white-washed block-houses lining the road down to the waterfront: stores and warehouses, the carpenter's shop, the machine shop, so practical and common-place and yet blending so beautifully into the background of palms and thickets.

Although the tide was in now, curling across the sands almost to the grass, the motor launch was about ten yards out. The water was so shallow that Jassy could see the bottom glistening under the ripples. To the north of the beach, hidden from the green by other workshops, a short iron jetty thrust out into the lagoon with a miniature railway line of wheelbarrow trucks running back along a narrow slope to a big shed; to the south the outline of the boatyard loomed like a huge barn, its shingled outer wall festooned with nets and cordage hung out to dry.

Wading out through the shallows, Tao handed Eta into the launch and came back to carry Ana. Ray and Betty had caught up with them, and he swung her high in the air and splashed off after Tao, saying severely: "If you don't stop larking about, I'll dump you right here in the water!"

Noticing that Ben had become involved in last-minute instructions to some men on the beach, Jassy quickly shook the doctor's hand and gave Miss Jones a slight hug. "Goodbye, it was wonderful meeting you."

"Not goodbye, dear, good night. Have a good rest." She patted Jassy's hand.

Before either of them could prevent it Jassy gathered her skirt against her and walked into the shallows. The sand swamped her sandals as the tide washed over her feet. She didn't care: she was determined to reach the launch on her own—unless Ray came back to help her. The water was soon above her ankles, creeping up to her knees, but she plunged on with her head down, shivering a little as she peered into the shallows, knowing that the clear water could be deceptive about depth and terrified that she might stumble and fall flat on her face. She felt as though she were walking fully-dressed into the sea to get away from Ben Lanyard.

"Jassy!" The imperative voice pulled her up short and immobilised her completely. "Stay right where you are till I get there!"

She stood perfectly still, fighting a sense of helplessness and—yes—of relief too, but when Ben reached her she refused to look at him, saying defensively: "I don't mind getting a bit wet. I can manage on my own...."

"You can do as you're told." He swept her off her feet, his arms tense with impatience, and carried her out to the launch without another word.

Ray splashed round, helping her in as Ben went to the helm. "Those bare feet are too tender, Jassy-gal," he explained. "You could get septicaemia from coral cuts." His hand tightened for a second on hers. "Take care. See yer!"

Then the engine burst into life, puttering quietly as the launch cleared the shallows, rising to a steady whine as they nosed out into the lagoon. Ray waved, the backwash almost flooding into the tops of his black wellingtons; the people on the beach waved and turned back to the green. At first Ben followed a crazy, looping course she couldn't understand until she glanced over the side and saw that the launch was skimming along a passage of darker water on either side of which menacing domes and fronds of umber coral, flecked with the silver of startled fish, lay close beneath the surface of the lagoon.

In a few minutes the coral shelf dropped sheerly into the depths and the launch raced across the deep-water channel, sending an arc of white spray rolling out in widening circles behind them.

A cool young arm slipped under Jassy's confidingly. "Was it all right?—the surprise party? Was it as good as parties in London?"

"Oh, Betty, I never realised they would go to so much trouble just for me. I'll probably wake up tomorrow and find it was all a dream!"

She leaned her head back and closed her eyes, letting the whip of the breeze take her hair and her thoughts spinning away. She was so still that Betty sat in silence, resting against her like a contented child.

It seemed a long while later that the note of the engine changed again. Jassy stirred and opened her eyes; she must have been dozing. A moon-white sickle of beach and a mass of trees rose out of the sea in the half-darkness. Ben cut the engine; all that was left was the slap of water and moving lights and voices coming from somewhere overhead. The launch had been nosed alongside a landing stage of large coral blocks. Ben went ashore first, giving orders from the jetty, lost from sight for a moment beyond the swinging radiance of half a dozen lanterns. Jassy stood waiting with Betty, swaying with the rocking of the launch, until his arms came down and swung her up on to the coral beside him. He dropped to his knees, gesturing for light, and Jassy clung weakly to his shoulders, too bone-tired to think of resisting him, as he examined first one foot and then the other in her flimsy, thonged sandals under the beam of the lantern. He straightened up, steadying her.

"No cuts on her feet," he said. "Take her up to the house now."

There were two women standing on the beach above the jetty, silhouetted against lawns and trees and the long, graceful outline of an enormous bungalow in the distance. One of them was slight and young, almost as young as Betty by the look of her; the other was a towering old woman, in a black sarong and loose white shirt, with snow-white hair drawn up to the top of her head in a hard, round bun.

Betty raced ahead and flung herself on to the bosom that was as big as a bolster under the white shirt. "The party was wonderful!" she cried gleefully. "And she liked it! We were wrong, May-lee, honestly we were all wrong!—she's one of the nicest people I ever met!"

Jassy gazed in a vacant silence at the majestic figure and stern, lined old face. This was May-lee!

"Why you are so pale, like white rat?" May-lee boomed at her, enveloping her completely in her arms. "You are exhausted. Bed for you, come at once."

CHAPTER FOUR

JASSY spent the next couple of weeks at Lanyard's Landing on Heena Island, lazing around the house and grounds and trying to suppress a mounting sense of acute disappointment as day succeeded day. She tried hard to find some common ground with Ben Lanyard, but it was like pushing against an invisible barrier. His polite tolerance, his watchful, faintly sardonic manner would have become intolerable if she had ever contemplated staying indefinitely.

She had hoped at first to have enough freedom to explore Heena if not the other islands, but met with unshakeable resistance. Ben was seldom at home, except for dinner at night, and when she broached it to May-lee the old woman was adamant.

"Too much gadding about all at once is not good. Mister Ben is telling me you must go slow for a while. Rest and eat properly and not look so pale," she informed Jassy with grandmotherly but immovable firmness. And that was that.

May-lee was undisputed Queen-dowager of Lanyard's Landing. This was partly because she was the most senior of the dependants, but mainly a reflection of character, her imposing height and dignity and the full, rich booming voice which seemed to come from the depths of her large bosom. Betty had been in her care since babyhood; and as all the household staff seemed to be related to her in some way, including

Betty's companion, Bilkis, Reza the butler, Lala the cook, Toja the gardener, Tao and Ana, May-lee would brook no opposition or contradiction except from "Mister Ben".

It was a war of attrition. "Mister Ben says this must be done ... Mister Ben says that...." To begin with Jassy found her dictatorial pronouncements annoying; but in spite of all the talk about having come "home" she could not shake off the feeling that she was only a guest here and it was not worth antagonising May-lee for the short period of her stay.

The family property occupied six acres on the southern tip of Heena, cradled in the sound of moving water, the restless, ineffaceable rhythm of the sea. From the swelling tides of the inner lagoon across to the heavy rollers on the outer shore, the Indian Ocean pulsed against the island, a strong, unconquerable heart that never stopped beating.

Jassy's recollections of her first night on Heena were hazy. A walk up the beach, through clusters of ornamental palms, then over sweeping lawns as thick as a carpet underfoot, to the bungalow that dominated the darkness, like the bridge of a ship with pools of light streaming out on to the deck of the verandah. The building was deep with a high gabled roof of red tiles, and the shaded verandah seemed to fan out at one end forming a circular outer room, shaped like a turret, overlooking the lagoon. Jassy later discovered that the main bungalow had been extended at the back in two wings, on one side of which May-lee and the rest of the household had their apartments while the other wing housed the kitchen, store-rooms, refrigerated room, a generator for electricity and a pumping house for fresh water supplies.

Somewhere someone had freed a small brown mongrel, and the dog had come bounding out, fawning gleefully around Betty, giving Jassy a quick, exploratory sniff before he had hurtled off down to the beach in search of Ben.

The central *salle* of the bungalow had been no more than a passing impression of spacious luxury. A graceful arch divided the drawing-room from the dining-room, and the golden lamplight shed a soft glow on surfaces of polished wood and brass, draped silks, brocaded chairs, and carved ivories in an arched recess. The floor was onyx-marble, with a touch of deep crimson from Bokhara rugs.

May-lee had insisted on Jassy going straight through to a large comfortably furnished suite of rooms off the *salle*. Inside she found a friendly haven waiting for her, dim and cool in the shaded light and smelling sweetly of sandalwood and freshly laundered bed-linen. Her smaller travelling case had already been unpacked, and as she looked around, half asleep, Tao staggered in from an open door leading to a side verandah carrying two heavy, steaming canisters of water; he disappeared through another side door, a light clicked on, a swoosh of water tilted into the bathtub, and then he went out smiling.

To Jassy's embarrassment May-lee and Ana had hustled her out of her clothes and into the bathroom, and before she knew what was happening she was soaking blissfully in jasmine-scented water while Ana fussed over her, eventually wrapping her up in a thick, fleecy bath towel as though she was quite helpless.

And then she was at rest, leaning back under a

pink-flowered *razai* against a mountain of pillows in an old-fashioned bed of enormously comfortable proportions that had drugged her senses still further. May-lee had stood over her, supervising as she ate every mouthful of a delicious soup served in a delicate Chinese rice bowl. Laying the spoon down at last, she had rested her head on the pillows and immediately fallen asleep.

Ana woke her next morning with tea and toast. Eta had come tottering in, tugging at the *rezai*, demanding to be lifted on to the bed; and from that moment the visitor from London, who had been so reticent and solitary all her life, had been plunged into the busy communal life of an Eastern bungalow with all its friendliness, sharing, meddling and ever-open doors.

May-lee had examined Jassy by daylight without any concessions to politeness and pronounced scathing judgement. "What kind these guardians of yours? I would feel *shame* if my little one, my Betty-child, is so delicate and unhappy-looking like you." It was no use protesting or trying to explain.

If the old woman's nineteenth-century outlook proved rather disconcerting, Ana's quiet, persistent services had soon become a real embarrassment: helping Jassy to dress and undress, whisking away every garment she removed to wash and press, making the bed and keeping the room spotlessly clean and tidy. She even insisted on brushing Jassy's hair with long, sweeping strokes, fingering the glossy dark gold strands admiringly. Jassy's attempts to tell her that she had always looked after herself, as long as she could remember, were met with a pained, uncomprehending look. When she discovered that by rejecting Ana's

76

attentions she would be causing Ana to "lose face" in the household, she shelved her cramped English conscience and let her have her way, reassuring herself that it would only be for a short time anyway.

Everybody had helped her to get unpacked and settled, with an enthusiasm and thoroughness that suggested she would stay for the rest of her days. Everyone, with the exception of the King of the Castle, as Jassy began to think of him within a day of her arrival. Not that she saw much of him. He usually left the house at daybreak and did not return until late evening, unless he happened to be working on Heena, or on the neighbouring island of Venda which lay to the south across a gulf of beautiful, treacherous, reef-strewn water.

She soon realised that it was typical of Ben that he had not even considered altering his routine to entertain the guest in his house. His whole life seemed to be dedicated to the islands, and his reward was an almost slavish obedience and devotion from the Surans. He was considerate in his demands, he could do no wrong, and his word was law. The intense loyalty he generated astonished Jassy. He was an autocrat, but a vital, generous, sympathetic one.

All the more reason why she was secretly hurt and yet intrigued by his attitude towards her. The behaviour of this compelling man was quite unfathomable. Obviously he had set his mind against her coming to the islands, for no apparent cause that she could think of, but had grudgingly consented for family reasons. He had a way of speaking his mind that could be almost brutal on occasions, but not even he could flout the rules of hospitality by telling her she was not welcome in so many words. She had had to read it for herself in the challenging gaze of those unyielding eyes which made her wince inside although she somehow managed to stare straight back at him with a show of arctic indifference.

It began the first morning. Jassy had been wandering through the outer *salle* and the long, sunlit dining-room "catching up on the family". All the portraits delighted her, the earliest ones particularly; big, bearded men in high stocks or wing collars, brass-buttoned coats and rakish peaked caps, breathing the life of the sea, and pioneering women whose firm young features belied the softness of the draperies around their shoulders and the pretty drooping ringlets of their hair. Jassy recognised Ben's dark eyes among them, and the lighter blue of Betty's, and her own father's eyes, and other fleeting but unmistakable likenesses. She even glimpsed something of herself here and there. My ancestors, she thought, *mine*! ... still unbelieving and a little awed.

And then she had found herself standing in front of a portrait sketched in delicate pastels, hanging in a gilded oval frame on the pearl-grey walls. And if the girl in the picture had not been wearing a high-necked Edwardian collar right up to her chin and a coronet of thick, plaited brown hair, she might have been looking at a portrait of herself. Her grandmother's cool grey eyes looked down into hers. Do my eyes have the same expression?—Jassy braved the likeness unsparingly. So cold and reserved? Was it her defence against the world too? she wondered.

"So you've found her," a laconic voice came through the arch into the *salle* and the brown mongrel frisked jauntily into the dining-room ahead of Ben.

She was startled, glancing with a hesitant smile over her shoulder at him. He was standing with his thumbs hooked in the pockets of his slacks appraising her. His manner was far from cordial.

"It's an extraordinary resemblance," he said, "superficially."

"Superficially?" Her shoulders had tightened a little at his tone. "You mean in features but not in other ways?"

"You couldn't be less like her in other ways. Character, for one."

"Well, you would know," she shrugged coldly. "I never had the chance of meeting her, I was hardly even aware of her existence. Naturally you're in a better position to judge." She looked directly into the blue-black eyes for a second. "I suppose you've summed up my character as positively as you decide everything else. After all, we've known each other for at least twenty-four hours."

The sudden unpleasant brilliance of his eyes was like an electric jolt, reminding her of the first moment they met yesterday. "I've had you summed up a long time, my dear cousin," he snapped cryptically, and there was an underlying insinuation in the remark that she neither understood nor liked.

He turned to the portrait and studied it, pulling a pipe and worn leather pouch from one of his pockets and thumbing tobacco down into the bowl of the pipe with firm deliberation. "Your grandmother was a beautiful and very kind-hearted woman, but rather pious and reserved. And far too strait-laced to condone your outlook on life and the kind of situation you've got yourself into."

Jassy was so flabbergasted she dropped the icy pose. "What situation, for goodness' sake?"

"For *goodness*' sake?" he repeated, one dark brow arched up cynically. "We must have a talk about that some time!" He started towards the door that led to the back verandah, a brisk, businesslike host again. "Did you have a good rest? Room comfortable?"

"Perfectly, thanks," she responded stiffly. The conversation had made no sense at all, and yet he was not the type to say or do things without some definite purpose. She might not have understood what he was talking about, but she had got the message clearly—he didn't want her here, she was sure of it.

"Fine," he said, picking up his shabby jungle hat from a table by the verandah door and ramming it over his eyes. "I'm out on the job most of the time, but if you need anything just ask May-lee."

She said: "I'll do that." But he was already on his way, palms cupped round the match for his pipe, striding out into the back compound.

In a couple of days he was reminding his sister about her work for the islanders. Betty's contribution at this stage was to help in the Heena crêche and nursery school. An immediate longing sprang up in Jassy to ask to be allowed to help too, to enter into the life of the islands, but one look at the close-shut expression on Ben's face, as though he had guessed what she was going to say, and the words died on her lips. Almost as if he considered she might contaminate the Heena children! she thought with a stab of bitter resignation. Oh well, she wouldn't be here long enough for it to make much difference either way.

After that Betty rode off each morning after breakfast on one of the skittish little island ponies to the
main village on the far side of Heena beyond a thick
belt of nutmeg trees. The village, with its own small
harbour, served both the nutmeg and mace factory
and the market gardens of fruit and vegetables which
covered the whole of the north end of the island. It
was called Love-Apple Landing. Very romantic, Jassy
had commented laughingly. Very prosaic really, Betty
had explained with a delighted giggle, because "love-
apples" was just another name used by the old-time
mariners for tomatoes. Nevertheless, Jassy couldn't
help wondering if the name had had something to do
with Dr Ducase's waggish allusion to the Garden of
Eden on Heena, with his delicate wraith of a daughter,
Sophena, as Eve before long.

Left to her own devices, bereft of Betty's effervescent
company for part of the day, Jassy felt strangely uneasy and strung up. Part of her mind was always
listening for the sound of Ben Lanyard's launch on the
lagoon or the crunch of his footsteps on the coral
gravel outside the bungalow, playing on her nerves.
It was an absurd feeling she had never had to cope
with before.

One afternoon, resting in a bamboo recliner on her
verandah, half asleep with an unopened book on her
lap, she suddenly heard the hard, compact tread and
was so confused she almost bolted into the security
of her bedroom. But it was too late. Grabbing the
book, she held it open in front of her, trying to look
absorbed and unconcerned, blocking off that strong,
vital personality.

Ben came and stood over her, took the book out of

her hands and turning it round gave it back. He said, with a sardonic glint: "It's easier to read that way." Realising that she had been holding it with the print upside-down she flushed scarlet. For an instant she hated him with an elemental fury.

"I was hoping to find you on your own," he told her, using a sharp change of tone. Gone was the mocking humour and in its place a stern, uncompromising frown which made her stiffen. "Last night I heard you discussing your life in London with Betty, talking about someone called Tony."

"Tony? Oh, you mean Toni Lawler, my flat-mate. Yes, I was."

"I want an assurance from you that you won't do that again, Jassy."

"B-but why?" she stammered, surprised by such an unreasonable request.

"I should think it's perfectly apparent, even to you. What you do, how you choose to live when you're in England is your own business. It has nothing to do with Betty. She's almost childlike compared with youngsters of her age in London, and we prefer it that way. She's quite dazzled by your arrival," he admitted dryly, turning away to look out across the garden. "Because she's so eager and impressionable, try and be as circumspect as you can, for her sake if not for mine."

"What's wrong with telling her about—"

He looked at her; the taut jawline, the intimidating eyes cut her short.

"Just steer clear of the way you spend your time in London. Is that understood?"

"No, it is *not* understood."

"It had better be," he said evenly, and the determination behind the quietness was more daunting than any threat of violence.

A mute protest died on her breath as Eta came tottering out on to the verandah towards her. Ben scooped the child up high. She gave an enraptured little squeal, clasped her arms around his neck and buried her small dark head against his throat. Before Jassy had time to say another word he had carried the child off into the bungalow, presumably in search of Ana.

Thinking over his peculiar request, which had so bluntly become an order, the only conclusion Jassy could come to was that Ben was afraid that too much talk about the pleasures of living in London would make his high-spirited, impulsive young sister discontented with her life here. And what would it be like for Betty if Ben were to marry Sophena one of these days?—as the winsomely determined gleam in Sophena's eyes had made all too probable. Betty disliked Sophena; it was mutual. If Betty became enamoured with the idea of going to London, she would pester Ben to get her out of Sophena's way. And there was only one place Ben might conceivably allow her to go—to Aunt Dora's.

At the recollection of Aunt Dora's unsympathetic nature and oppressive discipline and the thought of what it might do to Betty's bright, loving, unfettered spirit Jassy sighed. Ben was right, though not perhaps exactly in the way he had intended. For Betty's sake she would co-operate by avoiding the subject of living in London as much as possible.

There were no more unexpected confrontations with

Ben, yet Jassy could not settle down to wholehearted enjoyment of this strange holiday. If I idle around Lanyard's Landing much longer, with nothing better to do than become edgy about Ben's comings and goings, I'll soon be competing with the dog! she upbraided herself ruefully.

Whenever Ben had to leave the mongrel behind, he would slump down morosely by the threshold of the turret room, looking nervy and neglected for most of the day. He turned soulful, liquid eyes on Jassy as she stooped to tickle the backs of his untidy ears and asked his name.

"Mee-Too," Betty giggled. "If Ben moves a muscle to go anywhere he's panting to go too, so we called him Mee-Too. If you were big enough you'd fill up Ben's shadow, wouldn't you, you sentimental coot!"

So would they all, Jassy reflected hollowly.

In spite of his ambiguous attitude she had to concede Ben's attractiveness, his potent vitality. There was strength in the lean, hard flesh on his big bones and he seemed to infuse everyone around him with his own confidence. He made most of the decisions and took the consequences. She had seen how gentle and indulgent he could be with Betty and Eta, how patient he was with May-lee's fussing and interference. Cunningly he had learned to handle the islanders with a mixture of command and consent.

Ben was certainly a staunch friend but a powerful enemy. His anger, when roused, was scarifying, as Jassy found out when she overheard him one evening on the radio link to another island where carelessness in covering a specially built refuse-pit had resulted in a plague of flies and endangered the health of one of the villages.

Whatever his moods, the vibrant quality of his essential being pervaded the bungalow even when he was away from it. He was never far from Jassy's consciousness all day long and she wished, fervently, that he liked her instead of just putting up with her.

The long dusky evenings were the hardest to sustain. Ben's talk was clipped and impersonal as they ate at the old oak dining table laid with damask, silver and crystal wine goblets. The atmosphere was charged with his presence. While taking coffee in the *salle* they sat around the wireless for the B.B.C. World Service or music from one of the myriad radio stations that jostled with morse and a babble of foreign languages on short wave. Jassy loved the mellow beauty of the *salle*, the sense of continuity in the portraits around them, the sheen of age on furniture brought piece by piece on sailing ships, but the feeling of being on sufferance marred her pleasure in it all and she was at a complete loss to know how to deal with Ben.

On one occasion she found herself subjected to such an intensely personal scrutiny that a hot tide of embarrassment flushed her face. Why did he watch her all the time? Why did he continue to look faintly incredulous or puzzled by her quiet, diffidently expressed opinions? She thought he was waiting for signs of the boredom he had so confidently predicted, and she set herself out to be as animated and friendly as she could, exerting a shy but very real charm, to prove him wrong. Sometimes he almost seemed content to spend the evening in the *salle* with them, and Mee-Too would stretch out at his feet, with his jowl on Ben's shoe, half asleep yet half awake for the slightest move. Then Ben would get up, Mee-Too would race for the verandah door, and as the tall figure disappeared towards his office in the turret room something went out of the *salle* with him.

The others felt it too. Betty and Bilkis would fetch out the Mah-jongg set and try and initiate Jassy into the mysteries of gaming with the exquisitely painted little tiles of Chinese characters and Flowers and Winds and Dragons. May-lee would sit for a long time with her mouth compressed disapprovingly, and once brought herself to comment dourly : "To Betty I am always having to say do not play so hard that you cannot settle down to work. But to him . . ." she sighed, "I will have to tell him, do not work so hard that you forget how to play !"

After a fortnight of this, when Ben had left, Jassy was very conscious of the exasperation May-lee could not or would not express in words, and tried to bring it into the open.

"May-lee, does Ben . . . does Ben leave like that because of me ?"

May-lee cast up her eyes and shrugged.

"But *why*, May-lee? What have I done to offend him ?"

There was an awkward silence. "I have spoken to him, but he is in a strange mood. He will not discuss. Only he says he has much work."

Jassy took a deep breath and was perilously near to tears. She had hoped that she was just being oversensitive about Ben, that he was a self-sufficient, very hard-working man, sparing in friendships, and that she had been reading too much into his attitude; but May-lee's gruffness and reluctance in answering seemed to confirm her own misgivings. She couldn't talk it over with Betty, and she could get nothing more from May-lee. The holiday for which she had had such hopes was slipping away in bitter disappointment.

As if sensing her unhappiness, May-lee leaned forward and smoothed Jassy's hair back from her face. Jassy could scarcely bear the sympathetic affection in her rough, wrinkled hand and shrank away.

"At first I was not wishing for you to come here either," the old woman admitted candidly. "A flighty girl is no benefit for him, and London is not such a good place, I think. But now I am wiser. You are a lonely, unhappy child. You need his company too and it is very bad that he should shut himself up like this." Her voice was fiercely maternal. It was the nearest she could bring herself to criticising her beloved Mister Ben.

Jassy shut her eyes tight against the tears. Pride came to her rescue as she gathered up her defences. Pity was the last thing she wanted—not from May-lee, not from anyone. And certainly not from Ben Lanyard.

She said, with an ice-cold return to calm : "Well, I won't be here to upset him for long, May-lee. Just till Betty's birthday—I'd like to stay for that, if he doesn't mind too much. I want to get back to London anyway."

It hadn't been true before—she had longed with all her heart to have things different, to be able to stay— but she would have to go back to England soon for her own peace of mind.

She had retreated into her shell and spoke with such detachment and conviction—"I want to get back to London anyway", anticipating that the old woman would repeat it to Ben—that May-lee shot her a surprised, frowning look. But before she had time to take Jassy up on it, Betty and Bilkis came back carrying the card table and began setting it up, rattling the bamboo and ivory Mah-jongg tiles on the green baize top and chattering together, and the moment was lost.

Jassy found it hard to sleep that night, thinking over the situation, and the muffled sound of a typewriter from the turret room, being prodded slowly with a halting persistence that made her expert secretarial fingers itch with impatience, was an added distraction.

Why Ben should resent having her around was past comprehension. That he would be churlish merely because she had wanted to come and see her father's old home was obviously and ridiculously out of character and she dismissed it. There was something else behind this feeling of tension, but what? He wasn't wasting any of his precious time on her, so the interruption to his regular routine had amounted to less than a day. And he was too dynamic and capable a man to countenance any outside interference in running the Estates; he had nothing to worry about in that respect, least of all from an inexperienced young girl whose very existence he had managed to ignore for years.

By morning she was still very unsettled between the need to get away from the bungalow—from Ben; and an equally imperative need to stay for as long as she could endure it to defeat his hurtful, incomprehensible objection to her unobtrusive presence in his household.

May-lee looked her over at breakfast with a critical

eye. "Why you are so pale again?" she demanded aggressively. "Not sleeping well last night?"

Jassy laughed it aside nonchalantly. "Ben wrestling with a typewriter! It was Ben, wasn't it? I longed to get up and take the wretched thing away from him and finish the job properly!"

"He's still learning," Betty chuckled, thrusting out two fingers and jabbing stiffly at the tablecloth in imitation. "Rita Gomez is his secretary at the Estates office in Main Bay, but he got so fed up with writing all his stuff out by hand here that he bought himself a fancy little portable typewriter in London last summer. He bashes at it on and off, but he never gets any faster! I think his fingers are too big! *I* could do better, but he won't let me touch his special reports, chemical analysis and things."

"I didn't know Ben was in London last year...." It had registered in Jassy's mind with wounding surprise.

"Oh, yes," Betty assured her cheerfully, "he goes to the London office for a week or two every other year now we have the airstrip."

He visited London ... he had been there more than once in the last few years ... he knew that he and Betty were her only relatives, and yet he had made no attempt whatsoever to contact her!

She said, with a little rush of vehemence: "If I'd met Ben in London I wouldn't have come—" biting the words off at the stricken look in Betty's face.

"He wanted to see you, Jassy, honestly, he tried. He saw Mr Winworthy and ... and Miss Winworthy each time. But you were away at school the first time, and then you were always on holiday or something, M-Majorca or Paris or. . . ." The breathless, apologetic little voice petered out.

And neither Aunt Dora or Uncle Cecil had thought it worth mentioning, was Jassy's sceptical reaction. Ben couldn't have tried very hard or impressed them with his concern. Uncle Cecil was always engrossed in his legal practice, and Jassy had not seen much of him after she left the house to move into the flat, but Aunt Dora would have told her about it some time—surely Aunt Dora would have told her? Perhaps Aunt Dora *had* said something on one of Jassy's periodic visits to the house. If so, it had meant less than nothing then and she had no recollection of it at all.

"I thought it would be fun to write," Betty faltered on, "but Ben said I wasn't to pester you. He said you had your own life to lead without bothering your head about a couple of strangers stuck out in the wilds."

"Betty, I'm sorry! I didn't mean I wouldn't have come to see you," Jassy stretched a contrite hand across the table. "I was just surprised for a minute about Ben actually being in London—I can't think why!" She smiled her warm, deep smile. "I wouldn't have missed coming to meet you, you little wretch, you know that."

"Nothing but talking, talking, not eating properly," May-lee interposed sharply. "Get on with your breakfast."

Ben's visits to London rankled in Jassy's thoughts all morning. Whether he had made any real effort to get in touch with her seemed doubtful. A very perfunctory effort perhaps—to be able to reassure Betty, and some of the others, like Miss Jones, that he had tried. Since he had not condescended to write and let her know that he intended honouring London with his presence, he could hardly blame her for being away on her hard-earned holidays when he got there! And what possible reason would Aunt Dora have had for not telling her when she returned that her cousin had been enquiring for her and had missed seeing her?

She walked far into the grounds this morning. Tropical flowers glowed against lush green lawns that spread out into a parkland of shrubs and ornamental palms criss-crossed with white coral pathways. Moist, heady scents from flowers and sweet citrus trees seeped right into Jassy's bones.

She seldom ventured such a distance from the bungalow because of the sudden heavy rain squalls which swept over the atoll on the trade winds. Now as she cogitated about Ben's behaviour the heat and her own bottled-up emotions began to make her feel a little sick. She was glad when she arrived at long last at the low white boundary wall of the compound and sank down on it, shoulders drooping, staring at the plantation of nutmeg trees that Great-grandfather Lanyard had introduced from Penang at the turn of the century.

The thick green graceful trees provided her with a distraction for a few minutes. Far away along the line of the trunks she could see women gathering the apricot-like fruit, pushing long, pronged poles into the shiny foliage and loosening the crop so that it fell into their baskets. There were a few windfalls of ripened fruit lying on the ground near Jassy. The reddish-yellow skins had split open exposing the lacy, wax-like pink aril covering a hard brown inner shell. She had learnt enough by now to know that the dried aril would become blades of spicy mace, and that nutmegs were the "seeds" inside the inner shells.

Jassy dug her heels restlessly into the dark, matted grass underfoot, trying to resolve her predicament. Curiously enough, her determination to stay for as long as she chose gradually hardened. She had a right to be here, and no one—*no one*—was going to drive her out before she was good and ready. She became doggedly determined about it, wondering if it would be possible to remove herself, bag and baggage, from Heena to the guest-house in Main Bay for the rest of her stay. Even as the thought came she knew that May-lee would raise the roof at the merest suggestion, convinced that the family would lose face over such a move. And they would miss her too, wouldn't they? . . . she herself? A trickle of perspiration crawled down her back.

All of them, except Ben! Her pride would not allow her to ask Ben why he disliked her, wanted to shut her out of their lives. But if she could get him to agree to her moving to Main Bay out of his way, May-lee would just have to accept it, whether she approved or not.

"No hat," said a familiar voice grimly behind her, "and no rain-cape!"

"*Ben!*" Jassy clapped her hands guiltily to her head, colour flooding into her face as she swung round, every nerve alive to that large, lean presence.

He had come up silently from the plantation, the tread of his boots deadened by the grass. Mee-Too raced out of the undergrowth, snuffling around Jassy's long, slim legs, wagging his tail.

She might have guessed this would happen, she thought furiously . . . no sound of his launch leaving early this morning, and no sign of Mee-Too at the bungalow. She had been too preoccupied to remember he'd be working on Heena.

"I didn't m-mean to come so far," she wavered. "Betty isn't back yet."

"Were you waiting for Betty, or for me?" he enquired bluntly.

She took a sharp breath, the chilly mask descending on her. "Neither, if you want the truth. I wanted to get away for a while, that's all. I didn't realise how far I'd wandered until I saw the wall."

His brows went up, a little sceptically. The next moment his battered jungle hat was off his head and had been plonked unceremoniously on to hers. He surveyed her for a few seconds, taking in the bleak grey eyes and prim mouth, the tenseness of her slender body in a crisp, sleeveless lemon-yellow dress, and her slightly tremulous hands as she pushed herself upright from her seat on the wall. For her part it was as much as Jassy could do to curb a childish urge to snatch his hat from her head and hurl it at him; standing with his legs astride, scrutinising her, looking her over with that lordly insolence that provoked and humiliated her so much.

"You'll wear it," he said with a brief nod towards the hat, as if he had read her mind, "however unfashionable it looks. Or else! And if you wander again without a hat or a rain-cape in this climate, I shall administer a judicious spanking."

"That'll be the day!" she retorted frostily in a pathetic attempt to snub such pretensions, which made no impression on him at all.

He glanced up at the sky. "Come on, town girl," and he turned away to the coral pathway through the grounds, Mee-Too frisking off ahead of them.

CHAPTER FIVE

AS Jassy walked home beside Ben she wondered despairingly if they could ever meet on personal terms without this frighteningly hostile cross-current. He was civilised and rational with everyone else—and so was she. But when they were together it took every ounce of nerve she had to match her pride against Ben's perverse and powerful displeasure. It was no less real just because he never said it out loud, and it cut most deeply because it was totally undeserved. He was the one who had created this awkwardness. She turned an indignant eye on him : unreasonable, pig-headed, self-opinionated creature! Why didn't he say something now? . . . anything, to bridge the ominous silence between them.

He strode on, his mouth and jawline hard; but as this opportunity of having it out with him, away from the others, might never occur again Jassy eventually forced herself to break the ice by asking in a strained, unnatural voice how things were going on the Estates.

"I thought it wouldn't be long before we got around to that!" he shot out dryly. "That's a marvellous act you put on, Jassy. The golden girl, talking straight from the heart. Very convincing. You've convinced half the islands and the whole of my household of your loving interest. I knew it was merely a matter of timing before you found the right moment for getting down to cases with me. Well, here goes," he announced scathingly.

Then he launched into a pithy account of the financial affairs of Lanyard Estates. Yields per acreage; assets and liabilities; sales figures, profits and dividends. She was bewildered, not understanding what it was all about. His tone was harsh and sarcastic. After a few minutes the implication that she was only interested in how much money the company was making penetrated through her bewilderment and needled her into annoyance.

"If I'd wanted an auditor's report," she interrupted icily, "I could have asked Uncle Cecil to get me one before I left London."

"I see," he threw her a cynical glance. "You've already assessed the prospects pretty thoroughly, the two of you. All you needed was a trip out here to have a look round yourself. Do you intend marrying?" he asked curtly.

Completely out of her depth in this extraordinary turn of conversation, she stammered : "We-ell, s-some day, I suppose." Words crowded into her throat. "Not that it's any of your business!"

"On the contrary, it's very much my business. Your marriage—and Betty's when she's old enough to decide."

"Betty's perhaps. But you haven't the remotest concern or responsibility in my affairs," she tried to retrieve her chilly dignity.

"Not in your *affairs*," he was deliberately insulting in the way he said it. "But in your marriage my responsibility is to Lanyard Estates."

She struggled to keep a steady voice. "Meaning what?"

From Harlequin…a special offer for women who enjoy reading fascinating stories of great romance in exciting places…

ACCEPT THIS "COLLECTOP'S EDITION" FREE…

…JUST FOR TELLING US WHY YOU LIKE TO READ ROMANTIC FICTION!

Please take a minute to fill out the attached questionnaire …affix your "YES" stamp…and mail today! We pay postage.

HOW TO GET 8 BRAND NEW HARLEQUIN ROMANCES SENT RIGHT TO YOUR HOME EVERY MONTH!

Simply check your answers to the questions on the card, affix the "YES" stamp to question 4 and mail today. We'll do the rest.

Receive the latest Harlequin selections...automatically!
Now you can enjoy the convenience of receiving 8 new Harlequin Romances right in your home each month!

Get all the latest books before they're sold out!
As a Harlequin subscriber, you actually receive your personal copies *immediately* after they come off press, so you're *sure* of getting all 8 each month.

Cancel your subscription whenever you wish!
You don't have to buy any minimum number of books. Whenever you decide to stop your subscription, you just send us a post card and we'll cancel further shipments.

Enjoy monthly copies of *Harlequin* Magazine...Free!
As a subscriber to Harlequin Romance books, you automatically receive a free copy of *Harlequin* magazine each month. In it you'll discover a complete full-length novel, a biography of a famous Harlequin author, special features on travel, arts and crafts, and much more. It's included with your subscription to Harlequin Romances!

Moisten this
"YES"
Stamp and
affix to card
before
mailing

FREE
"COLLECTOR'S
EDITION"
BOOK
DETAILS
INSIDE!

"Do I have to spell it out?" he countered irritably. "You own a third of the shares in this business and they're worth a good deal of money. Up to now Lanyard Estates has always been held by Lanyards—it's much more than a business concern, it's a community, a whole way of life for us here. Human and social needs come first, a big balance at the bank isn't important; or should I say wasn't important until you cropped up? When you marry you can sell right out. I've no doubt your—er—future husband will persuade you to sell at a handsome profit. And I'd be a fool not to try and safeguard the people of these islands against financiers getting their claws into the Estates." A pause, and then he added quietly: "I would offer to buy your shares myself, but I've sunk all my capital into building and equipping the airstrip."

Jassy was at a loss. She stopped and jerked her head up, staring at him helplessly. "What makes you think," she said in a thin, vulnerable voice, "that it would be so easy to talk me into selling my shares . . . to you or anyone else?"

He stopped too, looked down into her whitened face and the bruised blankness in her eyes. He seemed to hesitate and then his mouth tightened. "For Pete's sake, Jassy, stop play-acting. To a girl like you, turning your shares over to somebody else for hard cash to have a good time won't break your heart."

He might as well have struck her in the face. She felt ill for a moment and pressed her knuckles against her mouth. Resentment welled up at last in a distressed protest: "A girl like me? You know less than nothing about me! You've visited London often enough, and you haven't even bothered to find out! All your life

97

you've had everything, the family, the Estates, a secure place of your own. You can't even begin to understand what it meant to me to come here, hoping I might be needed . . . trying to find—"

"Don't be tiresome," he snapped, looking baffled and extremely angry. "I'm not taken in by your touching demonstrations of concern, not after years of complete indifference without so much as a word from you."

She wanted to blurt out that she had scarcely heard of the Lanyards of Sura until a few weeks ago, but his anger silenced her. She turned away, pale and defeated, all the rigidness gone from her limbs. She seemed to have lost her reserves of icy hauteur. Her body spoke for her in the dispirited droop of her shoulders and bowed head.

"God! Now the injured innocent!" he said with caustic exasperation.

Grasping her roughly by the shoulders, he swivelled her round and jerked her towards him with a brutal impatience that knocked the breath out of her. Unused to being manhandled, she began trembling violently. The physical contact changed him too, for his grip suddenly altered and his hands slid round, almost cradling her against his hard chest, his fingers spreading, shaping her back.

"Jassy," for the first time his voice was deeply troubled. "Look at me."

Slowly she lifted her head and discovered that his expression was as bleak as hers. His exploring gaze held her spellbound, gradually kindling with fierce intensity until the leaping confusion of her heart began to fill her ears like a drum and everything dissolved into a desperate longing to subside against him and let it all go. It took a supreme effort to wrench herself away—away from those insistent hands and the engulfing darkness of his eyes.

"What right have you to judge my motives?" she flung at him. "Do you think you have a monopoly of good intentions because you've spent your life here?" She burst into tears, words tumbling through sobbing breaths. "I didn't ask to inherit shares—I don't want them—I'll *give* them to you! No price-tags, a gift! That should satisfy you and put you back on top of this exclusive little world of yours!" In a frenzy of indignation she whipped off his hat and threw it at his feet. "I must have been out of my mind to imagine I could ever belong to the Estates, or you, or anybody else in this benighted place!"

She turned, tears streaming down her face, and started to run. Off the path, through the trees and across the lawns to the bungalow. From the shelter of her own side verandah she looked back. Ben was still standing motionless in the distance where she had left him, drenched by a heavy downpour that had caught him unawares.

She had a cold shower, changed into jeans and a bright sunflower yellow tunic, and painstakingly disguised all traces of tears with make-up before Betty got back for lunch. While they were sitting over a dessert of delicious, dark green, lumpy globes of fruit called custard apples, Ben informed them by walkie-talkie that he was delayed at the nutmeg factory and would not be in until late evening.

Jassy was glad of the respite of these hours before

dinner, feeling ashamed and humiliated at having lost control of herself. She had not given way to an emotional outburst like that since her childish tantrums with Mrs Pinkerton. Toby Taylor had not been able to provoke her to such helpless fury, but words had suddenly begun to cut like knife wounds in Ben's sarcastic voice.

She thought she knew now why Ben resented her, yet she was no nearer understanding why he had misjudged her so completely. If they had met a few times in London he would have discovered for himself that she was not a money-mad good-time girl. If only they had corresponded and kept in touch. . . .

Why hadn't he tried? *Why didn't I*? she fretted. Ben had made precious little effort to establish the relationship, and she had made none at all. All those years without a word from her, and then she had thrust herself uninvited into their midst as soon as she gained control of her shares. No wonder Ben considered her insensitive and avaricious—coming hot-foot to check up on the property to see what she could get out of it.

Looking back, it struck her how unnatural it had been, this lack of contact for so long. Apart from some distant conversations at Dora's coffee parties about the Lanyards who lived in splendid isolation somewhere in the Indian Ocean, Dora had never encouraged any interest or talk about Jassy's relatives. No family pictures seemed to have surived except an old snapshot of her mother and father which Mrs Pinkerton had found in a drawer and given to her. The break in Jassy's young life had been so decisive, and she had felt so separated in later years, that she had never thought of questioning Dora, or Cecil who had always had so little time to spare.

She shook off a sense of uneasiness about them; it was disloyal to the two people who had done so much for her. Cecil and Dora would never deliberately have cut her off from her family.

To have felt so deeply hurt by Ben's contempt was absurd, but the feeling persisted all day, and Jassy dreaded the inevitable encounter with him at dinner. She dressed and went out to the *salle* earlier than usual to avoid having to enter the room under his sardonic stare in front of the others. To her dismay he was already there, a drink in his hand, his long legs stretched out from his chair and Mee-Too sprawling at his feet.

He rose at once and came towards her, his eyes narrowed, a shade anxious.

"Jassy! Are you all right? You're looking very pale."

She nodded uncertainly, disarmed by the unexpected gentleness of his tone. She had a wild impulse to reach her hands out to him, to have the grip of his around them giving her reassurance, telling her it was all a misunderstanding.

Instead her glance fell and she managed to say stiltedly: "About this morning . . . I d-don't usually behave in such a silly, maudlin way. I'm sorry."

"No! I was hoping to see you before the others came out." He put his glass down. "It was my fault, upsetting you. There was no excuse, except that I find it difficult not to say what needs saying without diplomatic trimming." He came a step nearer, his forceful presence scattering her wits.

He was much too close. "Please . . ." her lips quivered as she tried to retreat, "let's not start that again."

He looked searchingly at her. He said softly: "You're a strange girl."

"*Why* am I strange?" she entreated, unsure of a new note in his voice.

"Just when I begin to think I know what makes you tick, you do or say something out of character." The dark, absorbed scrutiny held her.

"My own character," she sighed, "or the one you're determined to give me?"

Ben hesitated a second, his brow drawn in a puzzled frown. He said somewhat grimly: "If I find I've been deliberately sidetracked——" The frown lifted. His knuckles lightly ran along her cheek and the touch imparted a little tremor of pleasure. "Jassy, we've got to talk this over, find a way to straighten things out before we're both——"

"Oh, there you are, Jassy!" Betty's voice broke in as she whisked into the *salle* from her bedroom. "You know what you were saying about how I could wear the *sari* Chan brought for my birthday party sort of draped more in a Grecian style. . . ."

Ben swore under his breath and turned away to the cut-glass decanters on the cabinet, and Jassy shut her eyes for an instant, her heart palpitating a little, wondering what he had had to leave unsaid.

"Oh-h-h!" Betty looked from one to the other, the sparkle disappearing. "Did I interrupt something?"

"Don't you always?" Ben retorted, giving her ponytail a playful tug as he offered Jassy a glass of sherry. "Go ahead, chatterbox. Enjoy your party talk. The rest can wait."

Then May-lee sailed in, and Reza announced dinner, and the difficult moments were over. Ben was easier; his attitude had softened perceptibly, and for some inexplicable reason Jassy found this equally if not more unsettling than his stiff, uncompromising mood.

On Sunday morning they crossed the lagoon again to the church in Main Bay. May-lee accompanied them, resplendent in a high-necked, ankle-length mandarin gown of purple satin and a silver-grey head-shawl. Betty had put on a dress of candy pink cotton with a soft, round neckline and full skirt, and a jaunty straw boater ringed with flowers. Jassy chose a slim white piqué skirt and a white sleeveless tunic piped with royal blue. As Betty was wearing a hat, she pulled out a blue chiffon scarf and deftly wrapped it, turban style, over her gold hair. She slipped on a pair of shiny white shoes and short white gloves, and although her clothes could not have been simpler, and she wore no jewellery, her innate dress sense created a cool, restrained elegance that was not lost on Betty and Ben and drew a smile of satisfaction from May-lee.

Betty said: "Oo-oo-ee! You look as if you're going to Buckingham Palace!"

Ben said nothing, but as he helped her into the launch their glances met and the compliment so clear in his eyes brought a tinge of colour to her face.

Ben used his launch as other men use cars. He knew every tide, every channel and shoal of the lurking reefs as other men got to know the streets and traffic hazards of cities. Jassy watched him at the helm. Big

Ben, purposeful, and alert, looking spruce in a tussore suit, snowy edges of his white silk shirt accentuating the suntanned skin at his neck and wrists.

It was warm out on the iridescent tide of the lagoon. They passed a sailing barge skimming along the deep water channel, five oarsmen rowing on one side to add speed to the lateen sail. The helmsman was braced against the stern post casually steering the barge with his foot. Terns and sheerwaters wheeled in the distance and a lone frigate bird drifted towards the dark outline of Venda.

After the service in Mr Bender's small, square, whitewashed church he set off to visit parishioners on Miro while the others accepted Ben's invitation to return with them to Heena for lunch.

Watching Sophena, so delicately chic in a green trouser suit, so blatantly possessive, Jassy chose to ride back in Dr Ducase's launch with Miss Jones, May-lee and Mr Chandra and not with Ben. Honesty forced her to admit to herself that she hated the sight of Sophena clinging to Ben's arm, mooning at him, standing with him at the helm of the other launch. She had no intention of competing with Sophena in any way . . . she had no wish to do so. May-lee was obviously avoiding Sophena's company too. There was no love lost between the proud old Suran woman an dthe doctor's daughter, and Jassy wondered how May-leee would fare if Sophena ever became the mistress of the bungalow on Heena.

Lala had prepared a delicious lunch. There were glasses of chilled tomato juice and sweet citrus juice nestled in little dishes of crushed ice, bowls of curried crayfish, platters of home-cured ham and salads, and papayas from the trees in the garden cut fresh at the table to reveal the thick, juicy, golden-orange wedges of fruit covered with glistening seeds.

As they moved into the drawing-room for coffee afterwards, Jassy thought Betty was looking rather downcast.

"Anything wrong, Bet?" she asked in a low voice.

"No-o-o . . . well . . ." she glanced round. Sophena was at a safe distance, settling herself in a deep chair with great care not to disarrange her suit. Betty said hurriedly : "Sophena doesn't think I ought to wear a *sari* at my party. She says it's not 'appropriate'— whatever that means. I ought to keep up Ben's position and wear a proper dress. I—I can't do that . . . I mean, it would hurt Chan's feelings after all the trouble he took. . . ." She bit her lip and added : "I wish Sophena wouldn't always butt in a-and spoil things."

Jassy held back a little surge of irritation and whispered confidently : "Nonsense ! Sophena doesn't know the wonderful things we're going to do with that *sari*, Betsy. A special kind of dress that'll please Chan too."

Betty's young face brightened, like a child with a sudden secret, and as Miss Jones came and joined them she said eagerly : "Like to see what Chan brought for my birthday, Jonesy? Come into my room when you've had coffee."

Jassy turned away to take her cup. Sophena's tactlessness was incomprehensible. Surely she could appreciate the little courtesies and obligations that went with being a Lanyard in the Suran islands? She, who seemed always to be concerned with what was "appropriate", would have to learn the important nuances of what was *right* at certain times in certain places if she hoped to become the wife of the master of the islands. Betty was bred to it and knew these things instinctively. Confusing the child with her own conventional notions of gentility—Sophena should know better! thought Jassy snappishly.

The men became involved in a technical discussion of various types of executive jets for private airlines, and Sophena was soon openly bored and restive without Ben's undivided attention. Betty took Miss Jones off to her room to see the *sari*, and when May-lee had finished presiding over the coffee service she retired for her siesta. This was the signal for Sophena to lean towards Jassy, pursing her mouth and shrugging expressively.

"I'm glad she has gone, now we can talk. May-lee is always *de trop*, but what can one do? Ben is too free with his servants. One of these days," her voice dropped confidentially, "she will have to move, somewhere else, anywhere else! I shall insist."

You'll insist!—the words remained unspoken, but Jassy had clenched her hands until her nails hurt her palms. Yes, you'll have the right to insist, she reflected with depressing certainty, looking straight back at Sophena with a fixed, blank stare. Poor May-lee; banishment as a reward for a lifetime of service. And Betty?—what plans did Sophena have for ridding the bungalow of her uncouth young prospective sister-in-law? She soon aired them. "That old woman is a most unsuitable companion for *la petite*, but it is not too late, I think. I have told Ben many times that he should send Betty to a finishing school now. I know of a very fine one near Geneva." Sophena was being earnest and sweetly reasonable. "They will teach her *la politesse*, and the art of dress, and introduce her to a good class of young man. Such an opportunity for her that you are here, Jassy. It could soon be arranged, and she could travel back to Europe with you. I have many important friends in Geneva who would be glad to keep an eye on her for my sake. You would support such a plan for Betty's benefit, *chérie*?"

"Only if Betty herself likes it," Jassy replied, stiff-lipped.

Fortunately Miss Jones returned with Betty at that point, and Sophena made a great play of being luxuriously relaxed and sleepy now. She arched her fragile body to stretch her arms, displaying her breasts against the close-fitting jacket, and stifled a yawn behind her long, white hand, while her eyes flickered under her lashes to see if Ben was watching her.

He was. He rose to his feet and suggested that Betty should show Sophena to the green guest-room and make sure she had everything she needed; it was siesta time, and he must apologise for having kept the ladies when they were probably wanting to have a rest in the heat of the day; he had forgotten that Sophena and Jassy were not yet used to the climate. . . .

"I'm going to write some letters," Jassy said briskly, and turning to Miss Jones: "What about you, Jonesy? Come and rest in my room?"

"Well, we don't have much time for siestas in the hospital, but this is Sunday and I think I would like to put my feet up for a while."

The men went out to the turret room to continue their business discussions, and when she had installed Miss Jones comfortably on her bed Jassy settled down in the armchair in her bedroom with her writing case open on her knees to work on the letters. Except for the whirring fan and murmurs from the turret room the bungalow was silent. Jassy glanced up from her writing pad after a while to see if Miss Jones was having a nap, only to find the friendly birdlike eyes watching her.

"Do you have lots of friends, child? Are you missing them in this out-of-the-way place?"

"I have lots of . . . acquaintances," Jassy answered guardedly. "I haven't missed them very much, not really. Not yet, anyway. I have one good friend, my flat-mate in London, Toni . . . Antonia Lawler. I've been writing her a letter by instalments—a little about the life here every day—for Ray to take on the next mail." Something in the kindly, quizzical look Miss Jones gave her made her hurry on, filling the gap with words : "Toni and I were at school together. Then her aunt, who has a house in Chelsea, let us convert the studio into a flatlet for ourselves when we started work together on the magazine."

Jonesy was not to be put off. "And what about your young man?"

"Which one?" Jassy parried flippantly, with an over-bright smile. "If I write to one, I'll have to write to them all. There were six in the office where I worked!" She pushed back her hair with a quick, covering gesture, wondering what had made her say that, as if she was boasting that every man in the office was at her feet! "No, seriously—the only other letter I have to finish this afternoon is to Uncle Cecil and Aunt Dora; they used to be my guardians. Chan arranged a cable over the wireless the day I arrived, but I must write and tell them how I'm getting on."

"Dora Winworthy," said Miss Jones in a sad, reflective tone. "All those years. . . . Were you happy with Cecil and Dora?"

"They were very—generous," for some reason Jassy felt defensive because she could not respond with the whole truth. "They had a beautiful home, sent me to a private boarding school, gave me everything I needed. I owe them much more than I can ever repay, Jonesy."

"Good gracious, you make it sound like a wearisome debt!"

"Well, I must have cost them a good deal—in time and money. I took a job as soon as I could to relieve them of the burden, I couldn't be a charge on them indefinitely. I mean, it must have been quite a big outlay financially too."

She shut her lips tight against the need to pour out the other side of it, the loneliness of not belonging, the child looking for loving encouragement, the young girl longing for a sympathetic confidante she could trust.

To her surprise Miss Jones returned dryly: "I admire your loyalty, child, but if it's a question of money, you don't owe them anything at all. Your father's investments paid for some of it, and all the other bills were met by Lanyard Estates."

"Jonesy!" She felt stunned for a second.

"They didn't tell you? Oh, my dear girl! But that's the way it was. John, Ben's father, made all the arrangements after the accident to your parents, and when he died Ben honoured them all the way. Oh, yes, Cecil has been a good steward," she added tartly, "accounts in full, submitted regularly in his meticulous fashion."

Jassy thrust the writing case aside and got to her feet. It was as if the whole fabric of her childhood had come toppling about her ears.

"Jassy, Jassy, don't look like that," Miss Jones stretched out a hand. "Here, come and sit beside me on the bed. Did you really think John Lanyard, or Ben for that matter, would abandon you to other people's charity?"

"I h-had no idea. I just didn't think about it at all. . . ."

"At the time, Jassy, there was little else John could do. His wife, Ann, had recently died, and Ben was only about twelve or thirteen then. Cecil Winworthy was your father's executor in London, and John had to rely on his judgement. At least he could make sure you had all the care and attention that money could provide." Her small, plump, capable hand clasped hard.

"Money," said Jassy bitterly, "that's all that seems to matter." There was a painful silence. "Why didn't Uncle Cecil and Aunt Dora tell me? All that time, and not a word. I always felt I was a liability, an expense to them both. A nuisance! Always trying to be grateful, and trying not to mind. If only I'd known —Jonesy, I could have been happy, I'm sure I could," she cried poignantly. "Happier, anyway; a bit of pride and self-respect left, knowing I wasn't beholden to them for everything I possessed."

Miss Jones frowned. "Cecil probably left it to Dora to explain it to you as you grew older, and never troubled himself about it afterwards."

"What I can't understand is why she didn't," said Jassy wretchedly.

Miss Jones's eyes narrowed a little. After a moment she pursed her mouth and said ruefully: "I can—in fact I think I'm beginning to understand quite a few things. Dora Winworthy has had her own subtle revenge after all."

"Revenge! On *me*? But why on earth—?"

"For being *you*. Tom's child." Jassy was looking so perplexed that she continued sadly: "Dora Winworthy was once crazily infatuated with your father. Don't look so astonished, my dear! She was a very handsome, determined madam thirty years ago, and used to getting her own way; I remember disliking her when we met once just before the war. A vindictive girl, quite ruthless. Tom and Cecil were friends, and as his sister she saw quite a lot of Tom in those days. When he married your mother after the war . . ." she smiled wryly, "what are the words?—'a woman scorned is a vessel of wrath'. Poor Tom! He had to put up with a great deal from Dora, unpleasant scenes and bitterness. With such a malicious disposition I'm not surprised she never married."

"It—it doesn't seem possible. . . ." Jassy's thoughts were in turmoil, attempting to grasp all the implications, refusing at first to accept the unpalatable fact that Aunt Dora, the woman who had dominated her life with such austere self-confidence all those years, had been secretly working off the rancour and frustrations of an old love affair on a helpless, unhappy child.

Aunt Dora had been cold, almost indifferent in some ways; she had never offered Jassy affection. But the notion that this indifference had been a pose and her behaviour a calculated expression of hidden malice was a terrible shock. It came to her, as a wry afterthought, that she had never believed Aunt Dora capable of any strong emotions—love or hate.

Looking down into Miss Jones's scrubbed, pink, concerned face she knew she had been given the truth. Not only had Aunt Dora never mentioned that Lanyard Estates were footing all the bills, she had actually said that Jassy owed everything to her, and had often used it as a form of reproach. She began to ponder, despairingly, on what else Aunt Dora had deliberately kept from her and used against her . . . like not telling her about Ben's visits to London . . .? She wanted to ask Jonesy more, but the words stuck in her throat.

"Dear child," the sympathy in the faded blue eyes was comforting, "I'm so sorry to have been the one to tell you. Since the day I heard that John had accepted Dora's offer to look after you I've had misgivings about this. Dora, of all people, bringing up Tom and Valerie's daughter! Life has these cruel ironies sometimes." She sighed. "Cecil's regular reports about you were as much as we had a right to expect, I suppose; childish ailments, how you were getting on at school, where you were spending holidays. How he and Dora had done their best to dissuade you from leaving the protection of their home and going your own way, but as soon as you were eighteen you could legally do as you liked. Ups and downs, all put down methodically like one fills in a temperature chart. If we could have had some letters from you, telling us about yourself, how you really felt," her kindly glance fell away, making Jassy guilty and heartsore. "Ah, well," she concluded firmly, patting with her small hand, "the estrangement is over now, thank goodness, and our girl is safely with us at long last!"

Jassy rose from the bed, her head averted, not trusting herself to speak for a few moments. She desperately wanted to explain why she had not written letters, that it was not wholly her fault, but a stubborn, lingering sense of loyalty to the pair whose roof she had shared for years kept her silent. She had to have time to think, to get things into perspective. She went back to her chair a little dazed, leaving Miss Jones to doze until teatime.

CHAPTER SIX

TEA was by the swimming pool built into the shore and filled by the tides.

Betty and Jimmy Renton were frisking in the water, splashing each other like children, when Jassy and Miss Jones arrived. Ben's dark head was visible alongside Sophena's flowery bathing cap as he paced her with lazy, even strokes across the length of the pool, and as Jassy stood watching them Ray suddenly surfaced beside her, almost at her feet, water streaming off his head and broad brown shoulders.

Jassy had slipped on a swimsuit under cherry-red towelling; it took only a few seconds to peel off her beachcomber outfit. Her quick, deep smile went out to Ray as she stood peering down at him, all the graceful lines of her body emphasised by the sleek black swimsuit yet quite unconscious of how provocative she looked.

The gaze that swept over her long limbs was frankly, appreciatively male. He gave a loud, slow wolf whistle. "You really are a lovely lass, do you know that?" he said with a wide grin. "Why have you been hiding in London all my life?"

"Why have you been hiding in Sura?" she demanded in mock reproach, fluttering her lashes exaggeratedly and revelling for a few moments in this lighthearted nonsense.

"Because I didn't know you were around!" He put

a wet hand towards her ankle and, guessing his cheerful intention of pulling her into the pool, she backed out of reach, laughing at him.

Ray heaved himself out of the water and joined her, his own laughter full of that friendly warmth that always made her feel relaxed and unselfconscious with him.

He shook his head, the drops flicking against her. "Ge-e-e!" he said, "the years I've wasted!" He had turned slightly and his eyes strayed beyond her. His grin faded and the web of sun lines stood out against his tan. "*Ah, how the years exile us into dreams,*" he quoted wryly, and following his glance Jassy saw that it was lingering on Betty cavorting in the pool like a young dolphin with Jimmy Renton.

Involuntarily Jassy's hand went out to touch his arm. "Ray, don't take it to heart. Please don't be hurt ... I mean, she's just having fun. Believe me, soon she'll wake up, and really look at you, and realise—"

"No," he interjected so emphatically that she was taken aback.

Recollecting the hopelessness she herself had felt over Toby, she could sympathise. Strange how little she had thought about Toby in the last week or two. Strange, too, how close she had come to Ray on such short acquaintance; how easily they accepted and understood one another.

The commiseration in her upturned face was almost tender as she asked: "But why not?"

"Anno domini," he returned flatly. "I'm sixteen years older than her. Yep, I'm older than Ben, come to that." The grin came back to his genial features. It was on his mouth, but not in his eyes. "I've kicked about since I was her age, I've sown my oats—some of them pretty wild. I know what I want now, but she hasn't had time to shake the dew out of her eyes. Somewhere out there, in the great big world, there's a handsome young sprout who'll be just right for her. She must have a chance to look around and find out." An infinitesimal pause, and he added: "Most of all I want her to be happy, I guess."

"Oh, Ray," Jassy protested gently, "surely age isn't all that important? She's been so sheltered here that she'll always need an experienced man to take care of her, surround her with love."

"Unlike an independent Miss Jassy Lanyard?" he said, making an effort at the old banter.

"No, be serious. I have a feeling about it—I don't know why—but I *know* that if you give it a bit of time it'll work out."

He put a square brown hand over hers and pressed it firmly against his arm. "We had you figured all wrong before you got here, Jassy-gal," he told her gruffly. "I thought you would freeze me to death the day you arrived! But I reckon I've got you taped. Under that frosty pose you're sweet and gentle . . . and too darned romantic. And you have a heart a mile wide." To her surprise he brushed her hair with a light kiss. "Some lucky guy is sure going to appreciate it one of these days!"

Colour flowed into her face at a sudden ripple of laughter behind her as a dulcet voice said gaily: "Ooh-la, la! The so-cool little cousin from England works fast, I think. Be warned, M'sieur Lanyard, or your valuable pilot will desert you and fly off to London with her!"

Jassy dropped her hand from Ray's arm as if she had been stung by a trace of venom in the arch tone. Sophena! She turned slowly, as impassively as she could, unconsciously straightening to her full height against the other girl's slight figure. Sophena, small and fine-boned, enchantingly airy in a wisp of floral bikini and a cap of rose-pink petals. And Ben at her side, with his back to them, staring across the pool. Jassy's heart faltered.

Tiny skeins of water trickled down between the tensed muscles of his wide swarthy back and gleamed in the thick dark hairs on his arms and legs. He looked even taller and more aggressively masculine without the restrictions of a suit of clothes, and there was something so threatening in his silent stance and the erectness of his shoulders that Jassy was momentarily frightened.

Then he faced her, and the hesitant smile she offered him was immediately annihilated by a look of such concentrated disgust and antipathy that she was horrified. She turned pale. After the encouragement of the recent truce between them, the cruel rejection in that look robbed her of breath. She bent quickly to where her cape lay by the pool, fumbling for her bathing cap, pulling it on and tucking her hair in with shaking fingers.

Sophena raised an amused eyebrow. There was a swift, comprehending glance from Ray. "Lay off, Feena," he said rudely, well aware that the brusque familiarity would annoy her and divert her attention.

"Do not use that tone, you!" she retorted sharply. Recovering her aplomb, she said: "I must get out of the sun," and strutted away to the bamboo shelter.

None of this reached Jassy as she moved blindly to the edge of the pool and plunged in, striking out for the other side, drowning her distress in the turbulence of water all around her. What have I done now? she kept saying to herself, *what have I done now?*

The rest of the afternoon was an interminable trial for her. She did her best to avoid Ben, while he pointedly kept his distance as much as possible. What depressed her even more was that Ben and Ray seemed to be avoiding each other too. How much of her conversation with Ray had Ben overheard, she wondered dully, and what could either of them have said to offend him so profoundly? At the back of her mind was the nagging conviction that Sophena had deliberately precipitated the unpleasantness to score off her.

She took one of the recliners next to Mr Chandra under the bamboo shelter during tea. It was difficult when he commented, in his kindly way, that she was looking pale. "The climate is not suiting you here, Miss Jassy?"

Not the climate but the unpredictable moods of one particular person, she wanted to say miserably, does it show that much? Aloud, she said: "I don't think I've got rid of the staleness of London yet," and changed the conversation.

After such a painful, inexplicable rebuff her pride demanded that she let Ben know she had been unaware of the generous financial arrangement between the Winworthys and Lanyard Estates. She would give Ben her shares and shake off the whole wretched obligation once and for all. A straightforward business transaction in lieu of money—her shares in exchange for the many advantages she had enjoyed for eighteen years before becoming independent.

Uncle Cecil was a lawyer, he would tell her how to go about making the transaction legal and final. And once it was settled she would be free. Free of emotional claims, of Ben's wounding arrogance. Free as the air to get on with her own life at last, all debts repaid.

Later, she accompanied Ben and Betty down to the jetty to see the Sura party off in Dr Ducase's launch. Mee-Too snuffled around, suspiciously watchful of Ben in case he should be going off with them. Ray came to her then. Taking both her hands in his he said in an undertone: "Honey, I'm sorry! Don't let it get you down. I guess Ben's got the lines crossed somewhere, that's all." He looked hard at her. "Like he was jealous? Holy smoke!"

"Jealous of what? Don't be ridiculous." Suddenly she felt awkward and pulled her hands away. "I think I know what's troubling him, and I'm going to set things straight as soon as I can, this very evening, if he'll let me."

"Uh-huh," Ray chuckled. "Just give him the old one-two with that smile."

But she didn't get the opportunity. Dinner was a strained affair that tested her patience to the utmost. Even Betty, who could usually be relied on to bridge any sensitive undercurrents with her inconsequential chatter, was rather big-eyed and quiet. May-lee announced her conclusion that the girls must be tired and should go to bed early, and there was no arguing with her. As they sat down to coffee in the *salle*,

Jassy remembered: "Oh, heavens! I wrote some letters, and I meant to give them to Ray, but I forgot."

She was conscious of Betty looking at her with wistful curiosity. Her pony-tail flicked round as she hastily averted her head when Jassy met her gaze.

"You—you like Ray very much, don't you, Jassy?" she was confirming it in her mind, not asking a question.

Jassy detected something in her voice that raised her spirits for a second. So Betty had noticed them together and was a little piqued? It was heartening to think she might have provoked some jealousy in *this* quarter, and much more likely than that ridiculous suggestion of Ray's. There might be some hope for Ray if Betty could be brought to see him as a man and not merely as an obliging adopted elder brother whose affection she could demand at will.

"Yes," she answered warmly and truthfully, "I like him very much."

Ben's coffee cup clacked down on the table as he rose, jolting her back to the reality of trying to tackle him. The mood he was in, which was quickly communicated to everyone in the drawing-room, withered her. She tried to force out a request to speak to him privately in the turret room, but the words choked on the ache in her throat.

"Dr Ducase brought a message from Deshwa Das today, Jassy," he informed her abruptly. "He wants to meet you. The doctor thinks he's fit enough for visitors, and I've sent word that I'll take you to see him tomorrow."

He strode towards the verandah door as resentment

surged through Jassy at not having been told earlier, not even consulted.

"I'll be on Venda first thing in the morning, but I'll come back to pick you up. Eight o'clock sharp," he snapped, "on the jetty. And no messing about!"

Turning on his heel, he disappeared, leaving Jassy furious and the others staring at the door in astonished disbelief at his blatant discourtesy.

At breakfast next morning May-lee was fuming with indignation because Ben had been called out to the island of St George at midnight to cope with a quarrel which came near to bloodshed. Two young hotheads had secretly made some arrack by fermenting coconut milk, and having become roaring drunk began to brawl over a girl. The village elders had done what they could, but when the fighting spread and knives flashed they had hurriedly contacted Ben on the radio link. The mere threat of the presence of Mister Ben had calmed things down, but he had stayed there most of the night routing out the illicit still.

"And now this morning he is needed on Venda and gone off there," May-lee ended, fiercely angry about the unremitting demands made on him.

At five to eight a lonely figure stood by the lagoon watching the swelling curve of a lateen sail in the distance. She had on the cool pink dress she wore on the day of her arrival, her face shaded by the floppy straw hat.

Jassy saw the launch zig-zagging with miraculous speed through the tumble of shoal water this side of Venda, and a few minutes later it was throbbing up to the jetty. With flutterings in her stomach, and apprehension in her eyes, she went over the coral blocks to meet Ben. The tide was down so that the level of the launch was below the jetty, and he came to the side holding his arms out to swing her down beside him. In spite of a busy, sleepless night and doing three hours' work on Venda already, he showed no sign of fatigue, but when his hands went under her arms, lifting her effortlessly over the side, and she was looking directly into his face, she saw that there were white lines around his hard, set mouth. His glance was devoid of expression. That in itself was something of a relief after the raw disgust which he had exhibited the day before. He's preoccupied, she thought guardedly, but nothing's changed.

And then, as his hands seemed to claim her and he lowered her slowly against him until her feet touched the boards, an incredible yearning swept over her to put her lips to his mouth and coax the hard, set lines away, persuading him to relent and soften towards her. It was a momentary aberration, blocking rational thought, leaving her scarlet and abashed and so deeply perturbed that she took refuge in stumbling away from him to bump down on a seat in the stern and sit with her hands clasped tightly in her lap, staring across the lagoon with blind concentration to shut him out. He watched her through narrowed eyes for a long, intolerable minute, then switched on the ignition. They had not exchanged a word, not even a civil "Good morning".

When he spoke at last they were well out into the deep water channel.

"Come over here beside me, Jassy," he said over his shoulder. "I can't hold a conversation yelling above the motor."

She was still alarmed by the craving for warmth and attention aroused by Ben's touch, and now had to contend with her own weakness as well as his harsh mood. The very thought of what Ben's reaction would undoubtedly have been, rekindling his abhorrence, his cruel derision of the "golden girl's loving interest", if she had yielded to that silly impulse, made her quail inside. She rose, very reluctantly, and edged up the launch towards the wheel, nervously brushing drops of spray off her face with the back of her hand.

Ben reached out to steady her, but she tucked her arm in, jerking pointedly away from him. She leaned intently forward behind the sheltering windshield and gripped at the side of the cockpit rather tensely. The constraint between them became almost tangible as she struggled to sink her pride and broach the subject which had been haunting her mind since the conversation with Miss Jones. The soaring speed of the launch eased down to a lower pitch.

He broke the silence without looking at her, saying in a level, impersonal voice: "I owe you an apology, Jassy. I was pretty rough on you yesterday."

"Yes, you were," she heard herself replying distantly, "unjustifiably rude."

"Was I?"—he was stony. "I'll agree it was an unpardonable lapse in the treatment of a guest in my house, but we'll differ about whether it was unjustified."

There was a cold weight at the pit of her stomach and numbness in her mind. She lifted her shoulders in a helpless gesture. "I know you dislike me, Ben, since before I got here, even before we met. You don't trust me either, though heaven knows why. But there's one thing I must put straight—I wanted to speak to you about it yesterday, but you were hardly approachable."

She glanced surreptitiously at him. He had been out all night and working all morning, but he was still scrupulously clean, seemingly tireless as ever. Whatever the demands on his time and energy, he had showered and shaved; there were no creases in the drill slacks tapering into his boots and his linen safari jacket looked freshly laundered, the crisp collar and cuffs turned back from his sun-browned throat and forearms. The battered jungle hat was a part of him.

"Well?" he said. His tone was not encouraging.

She took a short breath. "When I was talking to Jonesy yesterday she told me Lanyard Estates had been paying all my expenses since my—my parents died. I didn't know . . . it caught me off balance a bit. I always believed—" she hesitated, "I was always *led* to believe that I owed everything to Cecil and Dora Winworthy."

He glanced sharply at her, but said nothing, and she plunged on: "You've been thinking I'm very thoughtless and ungrateful, haven't you? That's how it must have looked from your point of view. But it's not true, Ben. All my life I've lived with a sense of obligation, a terrible, bitter sense of feeling that there was no one of my own, and nothing I didn't owe to the generosity of Uncle Cecil and Aunt Dora. I realised just how lucky I was; I could have been farmed out to a children's home. Oh, what I'm trying to say is that I did care very much about it ! . . . I was worrying about the wrong people, that's all. Uncle Cecil and Aunt Dora, instead of Lanyard Estates. I was concerned all the time how much it was costing, that's why I took a secretarial course, and moved into a flat, and tried to relieve them of the burden as soon as I could. . . ."

Her voice petered away at the keen, assessing look and the puzzled frown between his eyes. He said: "Are you telling me that Cecil Winworthy never told you about the agreement with Lanyard Estates?"

She stiffened slightly at the sceptical tone and was forced to abandon her scruples about the Winworthys. "That's precisely what I *am* telling you. Aunt Dora had no hesitation in rubbing in my ingratitude towards her as if I was ever difficult, the way children are sometimes. The worst was escaping from it, trying to make Dora understand I couldn't take any more—charity."

For a brief space the only sound was the pulsating engine as the launch nosed swiftly through the lagoon. Then Ben said curtly: "I'll write to Cecil Winworthy tonight."

"To confirm my story?" she said tiredly, abjectly certain that she had failed to convince him.

"I'll have the hide off him, if it's true!" His mouth was a tight line, and the steely note of suppressed anger made her shrink.

She rushed headlong into the rest of her plan, to placate him. "It doesn't matter now, Ben . . . please, listen to me for a minute. Now I know how things really stand, I can put it right. It's quite simple. . . ." She paused, striving to keep her voice calm and matter-of-fact. "Ben, I want you to have my shares. No, let me finish! It's the only practical, worthwhile way to repay you for all I've had. This isn't a gift.

125

Fair exchange, instead of money, because it's rightfully yours. I don't know the value of the shares, and it may not be as much as Lanyard Estates spent on me, but it would be a good deal towards it, wouldn't it? You need the shares—and I want you to have them."

The launch slowed down and he switched the motor off abruptly. The sudden quiet was oppressive. Jassy turned her back to the panel and pressed hard into it, hiding a ferment of uncertainty beneath a calm, sedate exterior as she stood braced against the swinging, slapping water under the keel and waited for his answer.

He turned slowly to face her. She met his eyes as confidently as she could, with clear sincerity manifest in her own. If only she could read what was going on behind that dark, probing gaze. If only he would say yes ... now ... *now* ...

"You really mean it," he said at last, sounding nonplussed.

"I really mean it, Ben. I owe it to you".

Again that fleeting frown and perplexed look. He raised a hand and she shut her eyes with a quick, unconscious gesture of withdrawal. *Don't touch me*, she thought incoherently, *don't touch me or we'll never sort this out*. Nothing happened. She opened her eyes and saw that he was resting on his arms, glowering moodily at the distant shoreline of Main Bay. He switched the motor on with a decisive click and she felt the tense anticipation drain out of her.

"You don't owe me anything, Jassy," he said tersely, "but I get the point. I wish to God the rest of your behaviour was as easily explained."

"How do you mean?" Disappointment swelled into hurt. "I don't understand."

He chose to avoid the larger issue, saying: "The Lanyard women always hold their shares until they marry, you already know that. It was meant for the best, to provide for the womenfolk until they had husbands to support them. If they married into the family there was no problem; if not, the Lanyards always bought them out," and he concluded dryly: "The family was so close-knit when the Lanyard Articles were first drawn up, they didn't foresee a situation like this."

He swung the launch in a wide arc towards the Sura reef. As the bow ploughed a furrow of leaping spray across the deep water channel Jassy saw the dark, undulating shape of a giant ray, for all the world like a shadowy, undersea carpet being swiftly dragged away below the surface of the lagoon. The devil fish, they called it, and she suppressed a shiver.

"You haven't answered my question," she said as steadily as she could.

"Do you want it in good old-fashioned terms? Whether I like it or not, your shares in Lanyard Estates are yours by every right in the book. But not to give away as the fancy takes you. In the old days it would have been your dowry."

"Dowry? For heaven's sake! It's too old-fashioned to be true."

"Our forebears weren't geared to the wider implications of Women's Lib."

"So I can't sign them over to you. . . ."

"No, you can't" he flicked her a cynical glance. "But if it's any consolation to you, let's just say I accept your belated attack of conscience as genuine."

"You'll accept! Ough!" She clutched the cockpit. Such condescension! A flood of angry humiliation made her grey eyes opaque and her usually gentle mouth tight at the corners. "You won't give an inch, will you?" her voice was rising unnaturally high. "Every effort I make you twist into an insult. You talk in sarcastic riddles about my behaviour. Yesterday you looked at me as if I'd crawled out from under a stone, so much so that even Ray—"

"Yes," he cut in scathingly, "let's get back to Ray. By all means! You seem to have made pretty good headway there in two short encounters."

"Because he's a human being," she flared, "not an automaton with a one-track mind." This was getting out of hand. This was not what she had intended. And there was nothing she could do to stop it; nothing she wanted to do except get under his skin and wound him the way he was wounding her.

"You mean he's easier to handle. Easier than I am —or the man in London, by all accounts," he shot at her abruptly.

She was so astonished by the sudden oblique reference to Toby Taylor—*who else had there been but Toby?*—that the hot colour flowed over her, she relaxed her hold and lurched a little. "Have you a conscience about that too?" he said.

She was silent for a few seconds, trying to collect her wits. Who could possibly have told him anything about how things stood between Toby and herself? Of course Uncle Cecil and Aunt Dora had known she had a number of men among her acquaintances, but that was as far as it went. She had not confided any further in them, or in anyone else. A casual friendship, casually broken. Perhaps Ben was only guessing that there was—had been—a particular man in London.

She said woodenly: "It would help if I knew what you're talking about."

"We were talking about Ray Calver. It may be a game to you, flattering to your ego, but Ray's the salt of the earth, too good to be made use of as a temporary diversion to console you after quarrelling with this man you've been living with—Tony whatever his name is."

"*Living with*?" she echoed stupidly, her sense so blunted by the rough, censorious tone that for a few seconds she did not grasp his meaning.

"According to Cecil Winworthy you were breaking your heart over him less than a month ago. Your heart mends fast."

"Uncle Cecil said that?" she asked incredulously. "But how—when—"

"He wrote to me by the next mail after your letter arrived, urging me to get you away from London for a while because you were making yourself ill over a broken affair."

It was true, of course; she had been shattered by Toby's unscrupulous little game, no matter how good a face she had been able to put on it. The tremendous effort she had had to make to hide it from her friends —and most of all from Toby himself—had taken its toll. When she was alone, when there was no need to show a cool, elusive detachment, when she was tired and her guard was down it must have begun to show. That day in Uncle Cecil's office, as he was telling her of her inheritance ... she could remember now the weary feeling of meaningless existence as she listened, the unreality of it, as though he had been talking about somebody else. .... Uncle Cecil must have sensed it then.

Toby—Tony. Toni Lawler! *Dear God*, she thought, *how did we get into a tangle of cross-purposes like this?* And what right had Ben to jump to the conclusion that she was that kind of girl? "A girl like you"—the recollection of his contempt hit her again. A money-mad, good-time girl, living casually with a man, quarrelling with him, running away, finding someone else to play around with while she sized up the prospects for the future. ....

"No pretty speeches? No protestations of innocence?" he demanded mockingly, and it was so outrageously unjust that she was suddenly as cold as ice inside, retreating right into the shell that for a short, foolish while she had shed completely and laid herself wide open to another lacerating encounter. Never with you, Ben Lanyard, she vowed, never, never again. No more denials, no more explanations; he could think what he liked and she would never try and defend herself again against his incredible assumptions and unshakeable judgements. This ludicrous misconception was the last straw.

The irony of it!—Ben despising her, with Victorian vehemence, for being shallow and immoral, while the miserable truth was that she had been too fastidious and her guilelessness had almost betrayed her with Toby Taylor. A little hysterical giggle bubbled up.

He said caustically: "You think it's funny?"

"I think Sophena was right," she retaliated in frigid

desperation. "You *are* worried about me luring Ray off to London and leaving you in the lurch."

The quick blaze of anger he turned on her made her cower away inside, but she managed to keep a look of cool scorn on her pallid face. This time she could see that by deliberately imputing the wrong motives to him she had touched him on the raw. A taste of his own medicine, she thought. A heady recklessness filled her; a need to taunt him and feel his hard, punishing hands.

"Oh, no, don't tell me," she said with a chilly, provoking smile, "you're entirely altruistic, aren't you, Ben? It's the islands you're always worried about, and Ray's welfare. Never your own convenience. And Ray's much too young to take care of himself!" She gave a light laugh. "This feudal interest in the private lives of your employees is rather fusty nowadays, but very moving."

"Careful now, kitten, your claws are beginning to show!" he said, thin-lipped.

"No, really, I'm terribly impressed," she retorted, the smile still frozen on her mouth.

"Stop it," he said trenchantly. "Sarcasm doesn't suit your image, and it doesn't impress me at all."

"But I don't have to bother about my image where you're concerned, do I? You're so—so damnably omniscient you know everything there is to know about me already!" Her eyes blurred with tears, her voice shook with tension.

She could see that he was holding himself on a close rein. She was scared at her own temerity in goading him, and yet found a thrill of satisfaction in watching his jaw muscle tighten into a hard cord.

After a long moment he said in a stingingly smooth voice : "Don't try me too far, Jassy, or I'll put you on the next flight out to Colombo and leave you to work your frustrations off on somebody else." He eased the engine down as the launch entered the reef channel into Main Bay and for a few minutes all his concentration was on negotiating the narrow winding passage while all hers was bent on stifling the pain and despair that flooded her at his cold, incisive tone. Not only had she failed completely to put things right with him, but by allowing her anger and hurt to get the upper hand she had made the rift between them now wider than ever.

CHAPTER SEVEN

BEN drove round the green and turned into a narrow
lane behind the huge festooned barn of the boatyard.
As he spun the wheel over the corded muscles of his
arm touched Jassy. The contact made her draw away,
holding herself rigid in the cramped jeep. Within a
few minutes the lane opened out into a long loop of
crushed coral following the contours of Sura Island.
Soon they had left the lagoon behind and were facing
the open sea. A wild jungle of thickets lined one side
of the road while on the other scattered columns of
palms leaned against the trade winds. In the distance
gigantic grey combers swept in and broke in a roar
of spindrift on the outer reef before sliding into soft
emerald green water between the reef and the coast-
line of silvery beaches. Jassy clutched the floppy brim
of her hat against the sea breeze.

It was Ben who broke the silence at last. He said
in an unexpectedly persuasive voice: "Try not to let
our personal differences upset Deshwa Das, Jassy. He's
an old and faithful friend, and a very sick man.
Meeting you means a lot to him—as it did to the
others. Will you try to forget what I said and be
cheerful and friendly for a while for his sake?"

"Need you ask?" she replied through compressed
lips. "Surprising as it may seem, I don't make a habit
of quarrelling, or enjoy taking it out on other people.
I'm not as insensitive as you choose to think."

He threw her a brief glance, said : "Good!" ironic-
ally and left it at that. Jassy thought : Ben and his
islanders! It must have cost him something to ask a
favour; but he was prepared to let anything ride, even
ready to put up with her against his own wishes—if it
would benefit his beloved islanders.

There were fishermen out on the coral lagoon
working with a seine net between the shore and the
fringe of the reef; one end of the seine was staked
ashore and a pirogue moved swiftly over the shallows
paying out the net in a wide circle. Jassy could see
the weights splashing into the water and the floats
dancing on the surface. As she watched, the pirogue
returned to the shore and by the time the jeep was
skimming along the road above the beach the little
group of fisherfolk had begun hauling in the two ends
of the seine.

Suddenly a scream pierced the air; then shouts and
a long, rising wail of agony so appalling that Jassy's
heart stopped. Ben slammed on the brakes, hurtling
them both against the dashboard. He launched himself out of the jeep and was scrambling down through
the scrub grass to the beach before she had had time
to get her breath back. The shrieks continued at full
pitch. Jassy got out of the jeep too, gripped it and
leaned heavily for a few moments because her knees
were wobbling with shock.

When she looked down there was confusion on the
beach, Ben squatting beside a figure writhing on the
sand, Ben's steady, dominant voice taking over. The
screaming went on, ringing in her head like a night-
mare, making her so tremulous that she could hardly
stand. She thought, I mustn't faint—whatever terrible

thing has happened, I mustn't faint. She took a series of long, deep breaths and managed to pull herself together in spite of the jumble of horrific images that raced through her mind: the mangled, bloodied flesh of people bitten by sharks that she had seen in a magazine once. It couldn't be a shark, she heartened herself shakily, all the fishermen had been in shallows pulling in the seine net. And there was no raw flesh, no gush of blood that she could see from this distance. Only those heartrending shrieks that went on, and on.

Ben was coming back, striding up the slope. She could read nothing from his face and it was not until he reached the jeep that her wide, frightened eyes noted the greyness under his tan and the tautness of his jaw muscles. He looked straight through her, picking up the walkie-talkie and snapping out a call for the hospital and Dr Ducase. Words penetrated her bemused state: "Stonefish ... fairly high up in the sand. One of the spines pricked his foot ... physically tough, but too young to survive the agony if we don't move fast. We've got to pull him through the next few hours ... ten, fifteen minutes at the most, I've got the jeep here. ..."

He finished the call, looked at the beach where a cluster of men were struggling to lift the figure now thrashing about wildly in excruciating pain. The screaming had become such hoarse torture that she covered her ears with her hands in despair. The movement caught Ben's eye. He seemed to make an effort and swung round on her with glittering impatience for a paltry nuisance to be got rid of at all costs.

"Get going, Jassy. D.D.'s bungalow is another mile up the road at Clove Point. Tell him what's happened here, and make the best of it. Tell him I'll send Bunsi up with the jeep to fetch you later in the day."

She dropped her hands. She wasn't listening to him, all she could think of was the horror of the Suran fisherboy's piercing howls and the men staggering through the scrub grass towards the jeep. It took seven of them to hold him, three to carry his slippery, sweat-soaked writhing body and two each to control his flailing arms and legs. A great surge of pity and anxiety rushed over her, submerging her own shrinking feeling of revulsion. She became oddly calm.

She said: "Is there something—*anything* I could do to help?"

"You?" the contempt slid over her elegant form. "What the hell do you think you could do? Jassy, get out of here. I haven't time to waste."

"No!" she shouted back at him, as implacable a Lanyard as he was all of a sudden.

His eyes flared, but he swung away as the men came to the road. "Please yourself," he said harshly. "If you're too lazy to walk, stay put till we've got the boy down to Main Bay. I'll send the jeep back, but for God's sake keep out of the way now."

She stood her ground, without answering. Now that the men were on the road, the fisherboy's pain-racked struggles preoccupied her to the exclusion of everything except his desperate need. Ben got into the jeep, revved it up, backed slightly and then swerved it round to face the way they had come. He left the engine running. As they lowered the boy's feet to the ground, he clamped a powerful arm around him and held him in a vice, gesturing with his head, clipping out orders about the way he was to be carried to Main

Bay. He detailed some of the men to come with him, sent one of them off to Deshwa Das and another to break the news to the boy's grandmother. Jassy had to move closer to hear what he was saying above the din of agonised howling. Ben's chief concern seemed to be protecting the boy's head from injury during the ride to the hospital and he soon gave rapid instructions for laying him across their knees and shielding him from the sides. His strong voice inspired hope.

In that instant she knew her place and got into one of the back seats, bunching her skirt up into a cushion as much as possible and taking off her floppy straw hat to push down into a protective pad against the wooden side.

Some of the men were watching her dumbly, accepting without question that as a Lanyard she was completely, automatically involved in all this; but the fury in Ben's eyes when he saw what she had done would have soon crushed her at any other time. This time she looked back at him with unflinching determination.

"Please don't waste time arguing, Ben. You can trust me to take care of his head while the men concentrate on holding him securely."

A swift narrowing of the eyes, no more; she must have convinced him. The fishermen scrambled into their positions in the jeep, the thick-set, brawniest man getting into the seat beside her. Then the boy was hauled up and lowered across their knees. Jassy recoiled at the heaving, screaming bulk below her face yet instinctively threw her soft, rounded arms about his head and tightened them. At the same moment the man by her side grasped the boy's body, the man beside Ben bent over the back of the seat and grabbed his arms, the man squeezed into the narrow space behind them reached over and grabbed his knees. The jeep roared down the road towards Main Bay spattering the men left behind with coral rubble.

During the next fifteen minutes Jassy's thoughts were a chaos of distress as she struggled to fulfil Ben's trust. It was an almost superhuman task for them all. The boy's bare, wiry torso was dripping with sweat to which sand still clung, making his skin like emery paper. His black hair, reeking of coconut oil, was wildly matted with sand. His shoulders flexed and arched in spasms of raging torment, his shoulder blades dug into her thighs, his head pushed and strained against the clinging protection of her arms. His cries, muffled now by those arms, tore though her . . . so young . . . a mere boy about Betty's age.

Incoherently she thought: *he trusted me*, Ben trusted me; and then, with stabbing honesty: only because there wasn't time to argue. She threw up her head for a moment to take a deep breath, unaware of tears glistening on her cheeks. Ben glanced over his shoulder and she saw that his eyes, so confident and purposeful before, rested on the fisherboy with dark compassion. He bent over the wheel again driving as though the devil himself was behind him.

A little crowd awaited them in the hospital compound. From the shadowy verandah arches Dr Ducase hurried out, followed by Miss Jones, in a starchy white overall and old-fashioned triangular nursing veil, a young Suran nurse and two orderlies in crisp white jackets. Ben spoke to the doctor, then briskly to Bunsi to take over the jeep. There were more than enough volunteers to hold the fisherboy. Jassy had a last glimpse of his contorted face as they carried him away into the cool recesses of the whitewashed building. The sudden hush was almost as unbearable as the noise had been.

Bunsi helped her out of the jeep, his usually cheery countenance grim.

"Will he be all right, do you think?" she questioned shakily.

"The doctor will help with the pain—that is good. It is not the poison, Miss Jassy, it is the terrible pain that kills."

"How soon . . . how soon will we know?" She rubbed the wet smears on her cheeks.

"This pain is lasting for nine hours, ten hours. If he does not die of it. . . ." Bunsi shrugged expressively. "Mister Ben has given the jeep and I must go for his grandmother now."

Jassy walked to the verandah as the jeep streaked away again. Reaction set in. She was trembling all over and sank down on a bench. She could hear running water and the clink of bottles, and smelt the mingled smells of disinfectants and drugs through the wire mesh of the dispensary window. She looked vaguely at the blackening bruises on her forearms and listened to the faint echoes of the boy still crying in the distance. Stonefish, the lethal poisoner, burrowing itself so treacherously in the sand. . . . She shuddered and clasped her hands tightly together in her lap. She would never forget today.

The Surans who had remained outside came and sat on the plinth of the verandah near her, seeming to draw some kind of comfort from her quiet presence.

An elderly man offered to have his wife bring her some tea, and she accepted although she didn't want it. A while later he returned accompanied by his wife carrying some mugs and a large, battered teapot, very gratified at being allowed to make this little gesture, and everyone sat around her silently sipping hot, sickeningly sweet tea.

The tea put new life into her so that when the jeep came round the corner into the hospital compound she was able to go and meet the boy's grandmother. As soon as she saw the wizened face, Jassy remembered the old woman who had approached her on the green her first day. She was lifted out, handed her sticks. Jassy gave Bunsi a wordless plea to warn them inside first, and slowly led the old woman to the verandah to sit on the bench. Those eyes, which had looked at Jassy with such sharp inquisitiveness that day, looked glazed now.

She sat waiting, rocking backwards and forwards in stoical sorrow.

"Ay-yea! ... Ay-yea! ... my   boy ... my   fine, strong boy. ..."

"His m-mother and father?"

"His mother, she has already died. His father is in the big ship working to Australia. I am saying to his father, do not go from us. But he would go. What will he say when he returns? If my boy dies, I will also die."

She swayed and Jassy put her arms round her and held her close for a while. There was a touch on her shoulder. Ben was with them. The old woman gazed up at him. He smiled at her, spoke with infinite gentleness, then lifting her bodily into his arms, with Bunsi to carry the crutches, took her into the building.

It seemed to Jassy that it was hours before Ben came back, but time had lost its meaning. The sun was well over the trees of Main Bay and she judged it to be mid-afternoon. A flock of plump, dark pigeons foraging in the courtyard rose in a fluster of wings as he strode out on to the verandah. For a long time he stood over Jassy staring down into her face. Their glances held, and for these moments at least all constraint between them had disappeared. She knew she should rouse herself, get to her feet, but she was lost in his eyes.

"H-how is he?" she faltered at last.

"Fighting it out." His hands reached for her. "Come on. You look played out and you've had nothing to eat since early morning. I'll take you over to the guest-house, you can have a shower and a meal and rest for an hour or so."

"But . . ." she wanted to rest here, on his large lean body, "what about D.D.?"

"He understands. We'll see him tomorrow, if you feel up to it, or the day after." The sureness of the hands stroking her so soothingly flowed into her like a current imparting new strength. "Think you could walk over to the guest-house now? It's only a few minutes and Sophena's there. She'll look after you until I can take you back to Heena."

At the mention of Sophena, Jassy straightened up and shook off his hold, withdrawing completely into herself once more. "No need to trouble Miss Ducase. It's quite all right, thanks, I'll take care of myself till you're free to leave."

"For the love of Mike, don't start upstaging me

again," he said gruffly. And then, as she moved away from him to the verandah step: "Oh hell, he's messed your dress up pretty thoroughly."

"Do you think I care tuppence about clothes at a time like this?"

"No," he said quietly, "I think you care about people."

The old Lanyard house was a mellow, two-storied building standing in an extensive garden ablaze with orange and scarlet canna lilies. Ceiling fans spinning gently overhead made the central lounge an airy, pleasant retreat furnished with rattan chairs and tables and a scatter of colourful Persian prayer-mats on the polished wooden floor. Dwarf fan palms in gleaming brass urns were placed on either side of the entrance and at the foot of the staircase curving up to the gallery of the upper floor.

Jassy was shown into a tiled shower room behind the lounge.

The shower refreshed her considerably, and when she had cleaned her dress as much as possible, combed her hair into a smooth, gleaming fall, and made up her face, she was ready to meet Ben again with detached calm. But her heart sank as she came out into the lounge to find that he had now been joined by Sophena. She was wearing a loose kaftan of Java print that somehow suggested the informality of a négligé, her eyes blinked drowsily at Ben as she listened to what he was saying, one hand laid proprietorially on his arm.

Her solicitude was overpowering and almost more than Jassy could stand. Once averted from Ben, her eyes were wideawake enough to note every detail. Her voice was bland, full of commiseration. "So brave you are! Such ugly, discoloured bruises on your arms! And the state of your dress! If you had been less large I would have gladly given you something of mine to wear."

"Jassy could wear sacking and still look good," the crisp tone intervened, that tone which could make a compliment a bald statement of fact. A flush touched her cheeks, and Sophena's eyes narrowed for a second before she turned back to Ben with a gay little laugh.

"A typically masculine point of view, *mon ami*! Jassy knows better, I think."

Ben drew out a chair. "Come and sit here, Jassy. I've ordered for you."

The waiters served swiftly, attentively. As Jassy ate the fluffy omelette, full of deliciously curried vegetables, she realised how hungry she was. Ben and Sophena sat with her, sipping long iced drinks. When she had thirstily finished her own iced lemon and refused a sweet, the manager of the guest-house came forward to escort her up to one of the bedrooms.

Ben was lighting his pipe, watching her closely over the bowl, the flame of the match reflected in two leaping points of light in the darkness of his eyes.

"Try and rest for a while. I'll be back for you."

"M-mm," she was aloof and offhand. At the foot of the stairs, however, she asked haltingly: "The boy . . . you'll let me know if anything. . . ."

"Don't worry about him, try and rest."

Sighing, she went upstairs, Sophena exasperatingly solicitous beside her, with the manager leading the way.

She was shown into one of the smaller guest-rooms,

where the predominant colour was a cool, restful blue and shuttered double doors led out on to the upper verandah under the shady eaves of the steep roof. She felt too depleted now to bother with Sophena Ducase, but when she had taken off the crumpled pink dress, and turned back the silk coverlet to lie down in her slip, she discovered that the other girl had not left with the manager but was standing at the foot of the bed. For the first time in their acquaintance they were alone.

There was a subtle difference about the tiny, willowy figure, the way she stood, the waxen droop of her eyelids, her lower lip held between sharp, even white teeth.

"My compliments, Miss Lanyard," came the sugary, faintly sneering comment. "First the gracious visitor, so composed, such *sang-froid*, to impress him with dignity! Then the sex appeal flaunted clumsily with that lumberjack from Canada, to arouse pique. Then the plucky helpmate, so conveniently there, zealous to assist him with one of his nauseatingly dirty urchins."

Confused by this attack, Jassy stared back at her. "What are you saying?"

Sophena's teeth snapped together. "Do you think a man of Ben's vigour, his demanding nature, would find satisfaction for his needs with a wooden beanpole like you?" She gave a brittle, angry laugh. "If it were not for your shares, your presence would count for nothing, let me tell you. Unfortunately, he is obsessed with his position here, and he is not unaware, also, that these—these *peasants* are expecting him to make you his wife. Otherwise—" she broke off with a hissing breath. "Have a care, Jassy, I have not come all this way to this fatiguing backwater to have you interfering!"

Her palms clammy with shock, and quite at a loss for words, Jassy lay regarding her blankly.

"Don't look down your nose at me, you London typist!" Sophena's green eyes flashed waspishly. "You know very well what I am saying! It must be obvious, even to you, that Ben and I have—an arrangement. Now we will have to wait because he must decide what can be done about you. Oh, I have seen the way you look at him! You may have the shares he covets, but that is all you will ever have, so you might as well pack up and leave."

"Go away, Sophena." Jassy barely recognised her own thin, weary voice. "You have no power to order me out, and no right to speak like this. Now, please go."

Sophena's lip curled: "Ah, bah! Try matching your cold comfort shares against what I can give him, and you will soon find out!" and with a derisive snap of her delicate white fingers she flounced from the room.

Jassy's head was in a whirl, the pressures of the day crowding in on her. She could hardly credit that the brief, distasteful scene had taken place at all. Sophena jealous! If only she knew what Ben thought of Jassy Lanyard!—had it not been so humiliating, it would have been wildly funny. The bitter amusement melted in a sting of tears. And then the nagging recollection of the Suran fisherboy, slowly dying in appalling pain, made her own woes seem so futile and insignificant that she buried her face in the pillow and wept.

She dozed fitfully until a discreet knock and a voice informed her that Ben had come for her. Dressing hurriedly, she went down. Ben's face was unreadable, but she felt her expectancy drop like a dead weight.

Before she could speak, he said quietly: "He's still alive, Jassy—just. By the grace of God we were there to get him to hospital quickly, but there's nothing more to be done now, except wait." He scanned the bruised forearms, the faintly puffy eyes and pallor, and said anxiously: "Would you like some tea?"

She swallowed the lump in her throat. "No . . . no, thank you."

His hand, firm yet gentle, closed round her arm. "They're keeping me posted by radio. I'll take you home now."

After that, a wordlessness, no longer hostile but born of mutual anxiety, held between them all the way across the lagoon to Heena and through most of the rest of the evening. May-lee fussed over her, bathed her bruises with cologne, scolded her aggressively for carelessly spoiling her pretty dress, and then clasped her close to her large bosom with smothering affection. Betty, whose volatile spirit was quick to react, tried hard to enliven dinner with bursts of inconsequential talk, her eyes flickering to Jassy's face, but after a while she, too, lapsed into troubled silence.

Dinner over, Ben immediately took his coffee cup and a balloon glass of cognac away to the turret room. May-lee sat in her usual chair, crocheting, and presently suggested that the two girls should start on remodelling the *sari* into an evening dress for Betty's party, as they had planned. Out came the *sari*, a tape measure, some pins. For half an hour they made an uneasy pretence of being interested in draping the exquisite water-blue silk, hand-embroidered in fine silver thread. Neither of them could concentrate. When, at last, Jassy heard the radio call, the blurred sound of voices, she rose precipitately to her feet, scattering pins all over the carpet. She turned blindly towards the door. Betty started to follow her, but May-lee held her back in the *salle*.

The call had finished by the time Jassy reached the turret room and blundered in, forgetting all her reservations. "Ben. . . . ?"

He looked round from the radio equipment. "It's a miracle," he smiled, "as if we'd willed him through it. All over, bar some treatment ! He's resting now."

This was her true inheritance . . . not pieces of paper called share certificates, nor acres of land, nor dividends in the bank, but a sweeping tide of relief and joy for her own small part in giving a new lease of life to one young Suran and his grief-stricken grandmother.

"Oh, Ben !" her face was radiant.

Simultaneously they moved, without conscious volition, into each other's arms and Ben kissed her lightly on the lips. Then suddenly his arms tightened and he was kissing her again in a different way. His mouth was invading hers, shaping it to his own, compelling her into a state of mindless ecstasy. With Toby she would have been terrified by the convulsive upsurge of emotion. With Ben she wanted to be closer . . . closer . . . to become part of him.

He broke away so abruptly that she staggered against the desk. After an ageless moment he picked up some papers at random and flicked them restlessly through his fingers, saying roughly: "Do you expect me to apologise for losing my head for a few minutes?"

She stood with one hand over her throbbing heart, the other clutching the desk. Through benumbed lips she managed tonelessly: "I never know ... what to expect from you ... ever. ..." and walked out on him. Not back to the *salle*, but down the verandah steps, around the bungalow to her side verandah and into the merciful seclusion of her bedroom.

CHAPTER EIGHT

THE next morning a small, battered-looking tanker came in on high tide through the only deep water channel into the atoll and anchored off Sura reef. A long snake of a pipe was winched ashore and Ben spent the next couple of days supervising the off-loading of fuel oil at Main Bay.

Jassy was relieved. She needed time to school the ferment of mind and body Ben had aroused. Yet the hours dragged endlessly and the bungalow seemed empty and lifeless without him.

It was incredible, she reflected helplessly, what a few weeks of knowing Ben had done for her. No matter how much Toby Taylor had flattered and charmed her she had always held something back. Ben had generated a highly-charged atmosphere, rejected her overtures, infuriated her with his cruel accusations; but the instant his arms had enclosed her and his mouth was on hers, he had succeeded in obliterating everything except the sweet, vital urgency of giving herself up to him. Her shyness, her reticence, all sense of restraint had vanished.

To Ben, kissing her might have been a trivial impulse. To Jassy it had come as a revelation. What she thought she had felt for Toby had paled into a sentimental delusion. Starved of affection, she had longed to believe that Toby really wanted her, and had let him persuade her she felt the same way about him. His duplicity had shattered a dream and hurt her self-respect—*but that was all*! It was Ben Lanyard who had the power to exalt her or plunge her into despair, and had awoken responses she had not known existed.

Sophena must have sensed it before she was aware of it herself—and Ben was in Main Bay now, probably sharing every moment he could spare with her, thought Jassy with a sharp pang. She told herself she ought to leave on the next flight out with Ray, but she kept rationalising the need to stay. There was not much future in loving Ben, yet even the ordeal of having to conceal her love from him seemed a small price to pay for the few precious weeks that remained.

She decided to stay and see it through, and filled the empty days helping Betty to plan her birthday party, and put her mind to devising a gown which combined the graceful folds of the blue *sari* with a tiny, silver-edged bodice and flowing butterfly sleeves. Betty was thrilled and excited, and Jassy planned to wear her own simple ivory silk taffeta as a foil for the pretty confection.

She was brushing her hair after her morning shower when she heard the drone of Ben's launch returning. The hairbrush clattered. Ana gave her a slow, enquiring smile. Jassy looked quickly away and pulled herself together. It would be too mortifying if the entire household became aware of her folly in falling in love with Ben.

She was at breakfast with Betty when the moment she had dreaded and longed for overtook her. Mee-Too shot on to the back verandah, every inch of him wriggling ecstatically, and a moment later Ben had pulled a chair out and lowered his hard, lean length into it, flexing his arms with a satisfied sigh as he said : "Anybody missed me?" Everybody had. The place had come alive.

Caught in silence, with her whole being reaching out to him, Jassy kept her head bent and went on eating, thinking that every mouthful of the flaky fish Lala knew how to smoke so delicately over coconut husks would stick in her throat. Ben had already breakfasted before leaving Main Bay, but drank a cup of tea, responding to May-lee's fussing and Betty's questions with relaxed good humour. Jassy was painfully conscious of his powerfully built figure in neat gaberdine slacks and tailored bush shirt, his bare, darkly tanned throat, muscular forearms and brown, sinewy hands. She knew his eyes were on her, but refused to look directly at him.

As she always saw Betty off to the Heena crêche, she had no excuse for escaping when he accompanied them to the stables. He tossed Betty up into the saddle, patted the pony's hindquarters, and waved her off through the compound. Turning away, Jassy heard his voice coming up behind her.

"Aren't you going to ask after your protégé?"

"My—? Oh, yes," (how could she have forgotten?) "is he getting on all right?"

"He is now. Jonesy is bullying him unmercifully. I think he'll be glad to get back to his village."

She could hear the smile in his voice and laughed a little, curling her palms tight and keeping her head averted as they walked back to the verandah. He stopped by the step, put out a hand and stopped her too. The contact shivered through her. Suddenly shy,

151

she retreated into aloofness.

"I haven't thanked you yet, have I?" He turned her arm over and rubbed his thumb over a fading bruise, but his gaze was fixed disconcertingly on her mouth.

"Why should you?" she withdrew her arm carefully. "Surely the fact that he's alive and getting well is enough for anyone who helped him?"

Was there a faint sound of vexation behind her as she hastily ran up the verandah steps? His tone was almost as non-committal as hers as he crossed the verandah and picked up his shabby bush hat.

"D.D.'s under the weather again, so we'll have to postpone our visit for another day or two." He crammed the hat down over his eyes.

"I'm sorry he doesn't feel up to it," she responded woodenly.

This time there was no mistake, he was swearing under his breath. He said abruptly: "I have to go to St George this morning. Come with me?"

Taken aback, she did not answer at once. Her heart clamoured to reply, "Yes!...oh, yes, please!..." but the voice of reason demanded to know why she should subject herself to yet another distressing session of undeserved censure, which would inevitably happen if she was any judge if his change of mood in the last few minutes. But the urge to be with him, for any time he was willing to give, was too strong to resist. This was the first offer he had made to take her to the plantations. Perhaps—perhaps he wanted to apologise.

"Now? Well, yes," she agreed politely, "if you like."

"I do like." His big frame blocked the dining-room door and then he was gone, stalking off through the *salle*. She stood in a pool of silence. She went to her room and hurriedly collected her things, knowing he would be impatient.

When she joined him on the landing, knotting a bright scarf under her chin, Tao was there to help her into the launch. It rocked slightly as Ben followed her. Before she could retreat to a place in the stern, he produced her floppy straw hat.

"Bunsi found it tucked into the side of the jeep. I hope it's fit to wear. Bunsi's wife has been diligently brushing and shaping it up in the last couple of days. He wanted to return it to you himself, but I forestalled him."

His face was solemn, but a little muscle of amusement twitched by his mouth. Equally solemnly, Jassy removed the scarf and put on the hat.

"Is it?" she asked, tying the scarf over the hat, making a Regency bonnet.

"What?"

"Fit to wear?" She contrived a bland mask and met his eyes for a second. The darkness of the irises unnerved her. She could feel the flush rising and started away to the stern. Ben said: "No!" and she knew he wasn't talking about the hat. An electric tenseness about him scared her a little.

Still doubtful about his purpose in taking her to St George, she came back to his side at the helm in some trepidation, trying to think up a lighthearted rejoinder. Fortunately he switched on the ignition and the launch began to thresh the water restively and move off, so she fixed her gaze on Tao's dwindling figure and the small brown blob on the coral blocks that was Mee-Too crouching dejectedly with his

153

muzzle on his paws.

It was a glorious morning out on the lagoon and in any other circumstances she could have been gloriously happy by Ben's side. The tanker had weighed anchor long since and was already far down channel towards the deep water passage. She made an effort to ask a few desultory questions about it, but Ben appeared to be preoccupied with his own thoughts and she found herself wondering nervously when and how the next argument would begin, or whether he was going to refer to the way he had kissed her the other night.

Ben had turned south along the lush, tree-covered outline of Venda. As they skimmed past the island, Jassy noticed the grey walls of a large concrete structure jutting out into the lagoon. In her interest to know about all the islands her doubts were briefly forgotten.

"What is that? An old gun position or something?" she asked eagerly.

"The turtle pen."

"Oh, no! You mean you shut them up in there?"

He cocked a quizzical brow at her. "Don't you approve of the tradition of turtle soup at the Lord Mayor's Banquet in London?"

"We-l-l . . . it seems so grisly, penning them in."

"There are iron gratings on either side to allow the tide to flow right through, and the bottom slopes into the lagoon, so it's always below water level. They're caught only at certain seasons on the outer islands, The Sisters, and well cared for in the pen until they're needed. No worse than keeping cattle or sheep or poultry." He glanced down at the distaste in her face. "Mostly green turtles, Jassy, the edible kind, though we do bring in a hawksbill now and again for tortoiseshell. The islanders still like making knick-knacks from it, but there's not much demand elsewhere these days."

She realised that he was amused by her attitude. If one had to keep these helpless sea creatures for food, it was probably the most humane way of doing it. But she had no time to dwell on the fate of the turtles because Ben had veered the launch around choppy currents to the other side of Venda, into a secluded bay of ultramarine water. There was neither beach nor jetty for a landing, the jungle of thick, dark green manioc bushes spilling over into the lagoon in tangled masses. An alarm bell rang somewhere in Jassy's consciousness.

"Are you t-taking me to see the turtle pen?" she ventured, looking up.

"I am not." He cut the motor, his eyes suddenly full of intent.

She stood, petrified, as he very deliberately folded back the floppy brim of her hat. His arms swallowed her up, his chest walled her in. He kissed her deeply and lingeringly, as if he had every right, quelling all her attempts to repel him until she abandoned herself to blissful oblivion.

When it was over he said unsteadily: "I've been waiting to do that again for two whole days." With the tip of one finger he outlined her mouth lightly.

Jassy pulled away and sank her head on folded arms below the windshield, shaken by conflicting sensations—loving yet hating him for depriving her of her flimsy defences so easily and expertly.

From the depths of uncertainty she said in a tight, chilly voice: "Last time it was losing your head for a few minutes. What's the excuse this time? Making me pay for the privilege of an outing to the plantation?"

His face darkened. "What did you have in mind," he countered shortly, "a big seduction scene?"

Jassy straightened up, flushing to the roots of her hair, her eyes luminous with reproach.

"Oh, for God's sake," his expression hardened, "don't make such a tragedy of it. You've been kissed, that's all!"

Impossible to tell him that it was not the kissing but the fear that he had embarked on a game, like Toby, that dismayed her. What had Sophena said?—"You may have the shares he covets, but that's all you'll ever have. . . ."

Indignation stirred and got the better of discretion. "I don't like being used, Ben! Go back to Main Bay, I'm sure Sophena would be glad to oblige."

She missed seeing the speculative gleam in his eyes as the hardness left his features. Grasping her shoulders, he drew her close again and laid his cheek against her forehead. Treacherously her resistance began to ebb.

"I suppose you think I'm fair game," she protested desperately, straining away from him. "*A girl like me!*"

He gave her a little shake. "Stop throwing my words in my teeth," he threatened softly. "I know better now," and he cradled her closer still.

"What do you know?" The words came faintly because the insidious magic was working again and she wanted to press her face into his bare brown throat.

"My dear girl, the first time I kissed you I realised—" he broke off, slid his hands down her arms and took her hands in his. "Come over here." He drew her to a seat in the stern and sat beside her. "I told you we'd have to have this out between us, and now is as good a time as any."

The unhappiness of the past weeks still rankled. "Why bother?" she said awkwardly, trying to pull her hands away. "You made up your mind *years* ago."

"It would be more correct to say I let others do that for me! The mistake I made, Jassy, was in not trusting my own judgement. That day at North Point —you were so different in every way from the tarted-up little tramp I'd allowed myself to be conditioned into expecting that it set me back on my heels."

She suddenly remembered Betty, the spate of un-inhibited chatter coming back to her like an echo . . . "If you'd turned out to be some kind of Chelsea freak after all, I'd have died. . . ." And later, in the darkness on Lanyard's Landing, "We were wrong about her, May-lee, honestly, we were all wrong!"

Ben leaned forward, arms along his knees, holding her firmly by the wrists.

"Jassy, when you were a child there wasn't much we could do to keep track of you, except entrust you to the care of the Winworthys. He was your father's friend and lawyer, and his executor, and things were pretty tough for us over here after the last war. I first met Cecil when I went to England to go to university. You must have been about eight or nine then. I was at Cambridge, life wasn't too serious, and

I was having a whale of a time—thinking more about girls a good deal older than you to think about you much, I'm afraid!"

He flicked the tip of her nose with one finger and leaned back, and love swelled her heart as she imagined a twenty-year-old Ben, big and gangling, probably a bit untidy, impatient as ever, rakish. He must have been attractive even then, although nothing like as attractive as the mature Ben.

"I used to look in on Cecil Winworthy sometimes, whenever I visited Lanyard's London office," he went on, "because my father had asked me to. But I was more interested in hiking around Europe during vacations, or staying with Dr Ducase's relatives in Switzerland. Cecil invited me to the house to see how you were getting on, we fixed something convenient to Dora, and then I had a cable saying my father was seriously ill, and had to drop everything and catch a plane to Bombay." He dug his hands into his pockets and stretched out his long legs. "He died before I could get back. What hit me hardest was the time I'd wasted while he was struggling to keep going through ill health, and the colossal problems of being isolated out here, dependent on cargo ships. I went for the problems bull-headed, concentrated on the Estates and let everything else go by the board. It took some bullying from Nora Jones to jog my conscience about you. I wrote to you once or twice, hoping we might start hearing from you personally."

"But I never received any letters!" she asserted in blank astonishment.

He shrugged his big shoulders. "Well, as Cecil had so little say in your actual upbringing I tried a letter to Dora, asking her to encourage you to write. She said she had done her best. You were becoming so unstable and unmanageable, they were going to have to send you to a boarding school. It was a good school, I didn't see much to worry about and decided to let it rest for a year or two."

At this further disclosure of Aunt Dora's malice, Jassy bit her lip, a cold touch of premonition tightening inside her. "Go on," she urged in a thin voice.

He must have felt her stiffen. "Look," he bent towards her, "you want the truth, don't you, Jassy? Sometimes the truth can hurt like hell."

"Yes, I want to know . . . all of it."

"The year after we finished the airstrip I went to London on business. You were away at school. Dora thought a visit in the middle of term from 'such a personable young man'—as she put it—would be unsettling to a girl of your temperament. I didn't like the implication, but she was so purse-mouthed about it I let it drop, assuming she knew you best. On my next visit she told me you had pestered the life out of them to go to Majorca with some friends, you wouldn't give it up for me or anyone else and became so difficult to cope with they had had to let you go. My patience was wearing out, believe you me!"

Jassy gasped, clenching her hands in her lap. "And I never even knew you existed!" She faced him accusingly : "You believed her!"

A long arm gathered her in, cradling her against him; a strong, harbouring arm which should have consoled her but only added to the emotional turmoil.

"Jassy, it was impossible to form an objective opinion from here. I knew you would be coming into your shares and I owed it to the Estates to make one more attempt. As I hadn't your address I wrote to the Winworthy's again, told them I was flying over and wished to see you. Cecil was away in Birmingham contesting a will and my session with Dora was pretty rough. She said you were in the throes of an affair and had gone off to Paris with him—knowing you she didn't think it would last. There was a great deal more, as if you had outraged all her efforts to instil any decency into you, and I was given a convincing picture of a wilful, greedy, promiscuous, thoroughly unpleasant minx!"

"*How could she!*" Jassy buried her face, horrified by the extent of Aunt Dora's mendacity. She put her hands on his chest and pushed away.

"It was true," she said stiltedly. "I was on holiday in Paris ... with Toni. Ben, there's something you ought to know, now, once and for all." She looked up straight into the narrowed, mocking eyes. Catching her breath, she said fiercely : "Oh, yes, I shared a flat with Toni. A friend of mine, Antonia Lawler. Female. So there was no call for that—that sarcastic, over-bearing way you treated me, as if I was a grubby pick-up or something."

"Now she tells me!" was the sardonic answer. "Why did you let me go on believing it? Did it amuse you to make a fool of me?"

"No!" and then more quietly, "Of course not. I was upset about the shares ... and hurt." Her glance dropped.

"Try and see it my way. Dora's insinuations; Cecil's letter asking me to get you away for a while, 'from a most unfortunate liaison'—the pompous old blockhead," he remarked bitingly. Looking at her drooping head, he went on : "I was in no mood to put out the red carpet for an unprincipled little brat from the permissive society who would insult and antagonise the Surans, demoralise Betty, and destroy the peace of my home. I tried to damp down the flurry of anticipation, but in the end I had to go along with it and be prepared to pick up the pieces afterwards."

He eased up the brim of his battered hat, tipped it to the back of his head and rubbed his forehead. "And then you were here, Jassy. No brassy assurance, posturing, or double talk. No temperamental circus for being kept waiting at the airstrip. Just a quiet, dignified, rather beautiful girl from England, staring at me with smoky eyes from a face as pale and reserved as your grandmother's !"

She looked up again, holding his gaze with a questing little frown.

"Why didn't I take you at face value?" he responded dryly. "I suppose Dora's poison had been at work too long. I had to have time to find out if you were genuine or a devious hussy putting on an act to suit the occasion. You appeared to be everything I could have hoped for, for the islanders—the immediate sense of rapport was extraordinary, even with shrewd old-stagers like Chan and May-lee and Nora Jones. All I could find was a touching shyness, a warmth and humour that seemed completely natural when you were not aware of being watched, and a defensive withdrawal into icy politeness when you became self-conscious. Not even a consummate actress could keep it up indefinitely. I thought I might flush out Dora's Jassy by scaring you or making you angry, but what I got was a breathlessly stubborn display of character covering up an almost heartbreaking vulnerability."

This penetratingly accurate assessment brought two burning spots of colour to her cheeks. His own judgement! she thought ruefully—he was always maddeningly right! Then why had he—? He was telling her why, in an unusually constrained voice.

"That business about Ray Calver." He turned away, pushing the hat back over his eyes so that they were shadowed. "Chasing men was the only element of Dora's innuendoes that seemed to have some basis. After the party at the school-house you made a dead set for Ray, like a homing pigeon."

"Because he'd been so kind and friendly," she retorted, wincing at the tone. "It was so easy to talk to him, he gave me confidence when I was nervous waiting for you and feeling a bit lost."

"And that day at the pool, melting all over him. More cosy gratitude?"

"Ben, don't," she begged unhappily. "I'd been talking to Jonesy and learnt things I'd never known, never would have believed! About the Estates . . . about Dora and my father. . . ." Her voice faltered for a second. "I came out full of ideas about putting things right. I felt happier than I had for years. Ray was there, like an old friend, that's all. Besides, he dearly loves Bet—" Hastily she pressed tremulous fingers over her mouth, afraid she had said too much.

"So you know? Ray's the man for Betty. I've always hoped she'd feel the same for him, given time. There's no one I'd rather trust with her future."

"I'm so glad you approve!" she began, with a little

rush of eagerness.

Ben caught her chin and tilted her face with an unexpectedly rough movement.

"Are you?" he demanded, his fingers bruising her and his gaze acute.

Jassy returned the look with wide, startled eyes until his hand fell away. He said, with flat emphasis: "There was a man in London, wasn't there, Jassy?"

Hesitantly she nodded. "But not . . . not in the way you imagine."

"I knew that as soon as I kissed you."

An artless "how?" was hovering on her lips when he interposed quietly: "Tell me about him."

Jassy looked away, clasping her hands together in her lap in the controlled mannerism which helped to bring calmness. "His name's Toby Taylor. . . ."

Ben's glance sharpened. She said hurriedly: "Yes . . . Toby and Toni. I realised it too. I suppose the coincidence helped Aunt Dora to—to misrepresent things so easily."

"Tell me about him," he insisted.

And then she found herself telling him. About Toby's brilliance at his job, his gaiety and good looks, his endless conquests, his relentless pursuit of her. About her own naïveté in accepting his glib assurances and the humiliation of discovering that his sole aim had been to seduce her and that he had taken a bet with his friends that he would succeed.

As the halting admission, never divulged to anyone else, came to an end, a muffled oath exploded from Ben. He was blazing with anger.

"You need your silly, impressionable head examined!" he snapped in an exasperated, unsympathetic voice. "And as for that aspiring Lothario of yours, he needs the toe of somebody's boot in the seat of his pants. He would have had the hiding of his life if I'd been around."

Jerked out of any lingering sense of self-reproach, Jassy said crossly: "All right—I wasn't experienced or cynical enough to see through him at the time. But that's the way I am. I prefer to start by trusting people, as I hope they would like and trust me. I never had any doubts about Aunt Dora. I knew about Toby, but I thought he'd changed because he really loved me. Anyone can change their outlook. You have about me—haven't you?" she added tentatively.

The tension evaporated. "Yes, my lamb," Ben said softly. "Am I forgiven?"

She became flustered. The caressing tone brought an ache to her heart, and the underlying remorse very nearly betrayed her into turning to him with all her love shining in her eyes. But it was only remorse—no more.

She swallowed and said quickly: "It wasn't your fault. I was rebellious and obstinate. I left home. I saw Toby a lot. Enough truth to make it plausible."

"Venomously distorted by a neurotic, embittered woman. After a long talk with Jonesy I put in a radio-telephone call to Cecil last night. God knows what he was about, leaving it all to Dora. Too damn busy managing the money like a diligent little mole to see beyond his nose. He made a mistake in suggesting you come out here, Dora must have given him hell!" His eyes narrowed with a mordant glitter. "Cecil will never be the same again. Nor will the feline Dora!"

Jassy shivered and got to her feet, a bit light-headed

with relief that the misunderstandings which had cost her so much in misery had been more or less explained. The difficulty now was the way she felt about Ben. With the change in their relationship, it would be hard to keep him at arm's length. Kissing her had meant nothing but casual sensuous enjoyment for Ben. What had he said?—"You've been kissed, that's all."

She moved away to the cockpit, her back to him. She must leave the Suran Islands soon . . . very soon. She would not be able to endure the exquisite agony of foolish hopes and illusions Ben might evoke quite unintentionally. This closeness, this touching would become more than flesh and blood could stand. And jealousy, raw jealousy of Sophena would maim her.

He followed her up, the launch swaying a little as he came to stand behind her. "Can you forgive the Winworthys and Toby Taylor—and me—for the way we've treated you, and make a fresh start?"

She glanced at him, with a spuriously buoyant smile on her lips. "Let's forget it all, Ben."

"Where have you gone to now?" he gazed at her keenly, "and why?"

"Meaning what?" she returned with a blank kind of brightness.

"You're no longer close to me as you were a few minutes ago, you frosty, elusive young creature!" After a long pause in which she tried to find words, he took the wheel and switched on the ignition with a savage click.

"Very well, have it your way," he said curtly. "It's too much for you to accept all at once. We'll leave it at that."

CHAPTER NINE

JASSY was relieved as well as vaguely disconcerted by the easy way Ben assumed a casual, companionable attitude towards her as though nothing had occurred. He did not attempt to kiss her or touch her again, nor did he say another word about what had passed between them, and the fleeting notion that her panicky rejection in the launch might have offended him seemed so unlikely that she discounted it.

He became a model host, putting himself out to show her round the islands. She loved visiting the quiet aisles of the coconut forests and was fascinated by the speed and skill of the plantation workers husking the harvest, using special iron-tipped spikes on which they banged the coconuts, ripped the husk aside and tossed the nut on one pile and the husk on the other. In the nutmeg factory she watched the tight casks being lime-washed and packed with marbled kernels for export; in the fruit and vegetable gardens at Love-Apple Landing she discovered that hundreds of tons of virgin foreign soil had been brought in as ballast on sailing ships to improve the crops. And in the cinnamon groves on Miro she learnt how the aromatic, pale yellow inner bark was separated into "quills" and "featherings" and went to spice markets all over the world.

Life at the bungalow took on a new and poignant meaning for her, and during the hours Ben had to spend in the Estates Office at Main Bay she threw herself wholeheartedly into the preparations for Betty's birthday. It was the only way to stifle the haunting knowledge that Ben would be seeing Sophena every day. She tried once or twice to raise the question of giving Ben her shares again, and to talk about returning to London, but each time something in his manner warned her not to upset the tenuous friendship growing between them.

A week later Ben took Jassy to visit Deshwa Das. Betty accompanied them to Main Bay and went to the guest-house, to discuss the banquet to be held there, while they took the jeep around the coast road to Clove Point. Jassy, whose heartache was becoming unendurable as the days passed, screwed up her courage to tell Ben she would be leaving after Betty's birthday, but shirked it at the last moment.

Deshwa Das's bungalow stood in the shelter of palms and breadfruit trees. They walked up a narrow path between shrubs of flowering allamanda and blue plumbago, and Ben propelled her towards the door, a cool, open square of darkness under the thick overhanging thatch of the verandah.

Jassy stopped on the threshold, the brilliant sunshine behind her, trying to adjust to the dim light of the room, when a frail voice welcomed her in. Then she saw the thin, crumpled shape sitting in an old-fashioned bath-chair and compassion swept all her self-consciousness away as she crossed the room and sank down on a wicker stool beside the sick old man.

"A true daughter of Surya," he said in a soft, cultured voice, "bringing me lifegiving warmth! I have waited a long time to meet you, Jacynth."

"I'm sorry it's been so long too." She took one of the clawlike brown hands in both hers. His body was feeble, but his eyes were clear and perceptive. She smiled up at him. "What did you mean—Surya's daughter?"

"Ah! You may not know the old Hindu myths. Surya is the light of the day, the Shining Wanderer. The sun, child. As you stood at the door against the light I remembered the legend which says that the Suran Islands were given their name by sailors crossing the ocean centuries ago who saw the sun rising behind Sura and decided that it was the dwelling place of the Sun God!"

It was the oddest beginning to a conversation with a stranger she had ever had, and in a few moments she found herself answering questions, asking them, talking animatedly and basking in the pleasure lightening his haggard face. Half an hour had passed before she realised Ben had left them together to make friends. While tea was served her gaze was drawn to Ben consulting his old tutor with affectionate deference and respect on matters concerning the Estates.

Shortly afterwards Ben rose, anxious not to tire him, and went out of the room for a word with Deshwa Das's servants. Jassy rose too, but the painfully thin brown hand kept her beside the bath-chair.

"You have put new life into me, child. Come and visit me as often as you can, and I will conserve my strength so that I may be present at your wedding."

"W-wedding?" She shrank a little, trying to draw her hand away.

His sharp eyes probed her suddenly wan face. "Do you deny this? Come now! I have seen how your eyes rest on him, Jacynth, and his on you."

"Please!" she protested. Just then Ben returned and she managed to evade the old man's faintly troubled look as they said goodbye.

Walking with Ben to the jeep parked under the palm trees she faced her dilemma squarely. What with the embarrassing conviction among the Surans that she had come to the islands to marry Ben, and the observant eyes of people like Deshwa Das, and the crying need within herself which had no hope of true fulfilment . . . the time had come to cut the strings and start making arrangements to get away. She longed to stay, but she had to leave. *She must tell him now.*

She moved abstractedly towards the palm trees, scuffing at a fallen coconut with the toe of her sandal, trying to broach it without too much explaining. He waited by the jeep watching her, then took a step forward, frowning.

"Has D.D.'s condition upset you?" he demanded curtly.

"As if it would!"

"What is it, then? Out with it!"

She took a deep breath. "I want to go back to London. Do you think Ray could see about my tickets, flight connections and so on, when he goes to Colombo next flight? After Betty's birthday. . . ." Her voice wobbled and died.

This was followed by such a profound silence that it was like a thick cloak muffling her and making her feel a bit faint. At long last he said stiffly: "I see," with his jaw set in a dour line. And then in a cold, sardonic drawl: "So Taylor's fascination has prevailed after all. The proverbial absence making the heart grow fonder."

For an incredulous split second Jassy saw chagrin in the twist of his mouth.

"It has n-nothing to d-do with—Toby," she stammered.

"No?" he countered acidly. Staring at her, assessing the truth for himself, he suddenly rapped out with savage bitterness: "If you're intent on running away from me, Jassy, there's no need. I won't touch you again. Should you prefer not to live at the bungalow I'm sure Nora Jones would be pleased to have you move in with her. You don't have to go to the drastic lengths of returning to England."

He understood that she was running away from him, she thought wildly, and yet he did not understand at all. She averted her head, tears burning her eyelids. She was prodding restlessly at the coconut with her toe, totally lost for words, when another fallen coconut near her shifted and rolled. From behind the fibre where the husk had split a pair of eyes suddenly protruded and angled leg-claws scuttled round like an enormous matted spider. With a horrified shriek Jassy turned and ran, hurling herself at Ben and burrowing her head frantically against him, clutching him hysterically.

"Jassy!" he caught her close. "My dear heart, what is it? Has something stung you?" The whipcord of his arms tightened urgently: "Jassy, for God's sake, *tell me.*"

"That . . . coconut thing!" she wailed, every part of her shuddering with revulsion, "it's alive! . . . i-it has legs! . . . it's horrible! . . ."

"Coconut thing?" His hold relaxed slightly. He was suddenly convulsed with laughter and the tension snapped. "You little idiot, no need to be afraid! It's only a *cipaye*, a robber crab. They're always raiding for coconuts." He hugged her and said: "Take a look, it's on the tree now, and you can see its burrow."

"No-o-o. . . ."

Still shaking with laughter, he thrust his fingers into her hair and firmly turned her head. "Look at it."

Reluctantly her eyes sought the faintly pink and blue mottled body of the land crab edging its way awkwardly up the sloping trunk of one of the palm trees. She shuddered again and turned back to Ben, and his amusement was so infectious that she laid her cheek against his chest and began laughing weakly too.

Slowly the laughter died into complete stillness. Ben spoke her name under his breath. Everything had ceased to exist except their need of each other. His grip had changed significantly, and soon her own arms were clinging round his broad chest with almost desperate compulsion. She felt the muscles of his back tighten under her hands, heard the powerful beat of his heart and the husky endearments. The caressing fingers in her hair cupped her head and tilted her face up to his. And then the hunger in both of them took over.

It was a long time before he spoke again, murmuring: "You don't want to leave any more than I'd let you go."

Trying to think coherently, she drew away from him. Her face was flushed, her eyes enormous and revealing. "Oh, Ben," she whispered tearfully.

His lips strayed over her cheek to her mouth and she had to grasp his shirt sleeves to steady herself. He said : "We'll be married as soon as possible."

"*Married*?" she gasped. "But we can't. You can't—I mean—"

Eyes kindling angrily, his arms became hard. "What the hell do you mean, can't? You seem to think this is some kind of game, though heaven knows why."

She swallowed convulsively. "What happened with Toby, I suppose . . . how can I be sure? Ben, don't look like that. Don't be angry."

"What do you expect—measuring me up with that mountebank Taylor!"

"No! Oh, Ben, I don't know how to explain. You see, I . . . I thought you and Sophena . . . well, it hurt too much. So I made up my mind to go back to London."

"That indefatigable little charmer? I've known her since I was an undergraduate. More than ten years to commit myself if I'd felt inclined!"

She put a tentative hand up to his set face. Avoiding looking directly at him, she said with a little rush : "Why do you want to marry me?"

He raised an eloquent eyebrow. "Don't you know by now?" His tone was impatient. But there was still an unresolved corner of doubt in her mind.

"It's important to me!" her eyes implored him. "You've never once *said* anything!"

Ben's expression immediately cleared, and he searched her face with the passionate tenderness she had longed to find. He kissed her eyelids closed.

"My dear, sweet shorn lamb, have you been so bereft of love all your life you can't recognise what's happened to us?"

"I knew it was real for me—it seems ages ago. But

it could have been different for you. Just physical attraction."

"It was at first," he owned quietly. "I've wanted you since we met at North Point. I kept speculating about the man you'd left in London, and could cheerfully have planted my fist in Ray's face that evening by the pool."

"That's what he thought," she remembered with surprise, "you might be jealous."

"He was right, though I wouldn't accept it! The day we had to rush the lad into hospital I began to realise how much you really meant to me. The spontaneous way you barged into the thick of it, sweetheart, quite ready to go through hell with the poor little devil. The way you sat it out patiently afterwards, worn out but still sparky enough to snap my head off about your messy dress!" His lips were very gentle. "I knew then you belonged here, Jassy. I wanted you to belong to me. Not just to make love to you but to share my life. Once we'd cleared up the misunderstandings it should have been plain sailing— I was so damned sure you felt the way I did. But you became rather confused and edgy and it seemed best not to rush you. I wouldn't force my attentions on any woman. I had to be sure you wanted them, and you gave no sign."

She pressed eager, contrite lips to the base of his throat above the open collar of his bush shirt with such electrifying effect that the breath was crushed out of her and her head fell back on his arm.

The heat of the sun, the pressure of Ben's body, the dark, demanding intensity of his eyes rekindled her senses. Her heart started scurrying again, leaping from her ribs to the pulse in her throat. There was no more gentleness, only the fierce, instinctive emotion they shared making them oblivious of everything but each other.

"I want you," he groaned. "I need you. Are you going to marry me or not?"

An exultant feeling gripped her at the knowledge of her own power to rouse him. Gazing back at him provocatively between her lashes, she said hazily: "I'll think about it."

"Well, here's something to think about!" he said roughly, bringing his head down and with his possessive mouth and persuasive hands driving any lingering doubts and all rational thought clear out of her mind.

On the way back to Main Bay Jassy hesitantly asked Ben not to say anything yet. "Betty's so excited about her birthday. Coming of age is a landmark. It's her big day, and it would be a shame to—to—"

"Steal her glory?" he sighed exasperatedly. "All right, no announcement till afterwards. She'll have her day of glory without distractions."

But Betty was far from enjoying her glory when they entered the lounge of the guest-house. She was sitting at a table, eyes sparkling with defiance and high spots of colour on her cheekbones. Beside her sat Sophena curled up as gracefully as a kitten in one of the rattan chairs. The disparaging tone of her voice ceased abruptly as she rose and went across to Ben, patting her hair, her doe eyes flickering up to his in a demure welcome.

"You have been so long, *mon cher*, I thought you had forgotten me," she pouted, disposing of Jassy's presence with a brief, mechanical smile.

"Has Betty been boring you?" he answered, and for the first time Jassy became aware of a steely thread of irony she had always missed before.

"What's the matter, Bet?" she asked softly against the dulcet flow of Sophena's determined monopoly of Ben's attention.

"She's been interfering with everything I tried to arrange for the banquet, and criticising me, and what Ben has to put up with! On and on and on!"

Ben's voice broke in: "I have to go over to the Estates Office to sign some letters. Ready to leave in about fifteen minutes, you two?"

"Fine," Jassy smiled at him. His hands were busy filling his pipe, but his gaze clung to hers with an intimacy that was unmistakable. A tell-tale rush of colour flooded her face. Sophena glanced over her shoulder under narrowed lids and Jassy turned hastily to Betty as Ben strode out of the room.

"I'll keep Sophena talking until Ben gets back," she whispered. "You go and tell the manager exactly what you want for your party, regardless of her opinions. It's *your* special day. Go on, Bet, scoot!"

Betty hugged her swiftly and whirled off to the office behind the lounge.

For about half a second Sophena stared at Jassy, her small teeth showing white and sharp against her lower lip, then she sauntered over and sank into a chair again and carefully arranged the folds of the saffron-coloured kaftan, strikingly embroidered in black, which she was wearing. Jassy took a seat at the other side of the table. Secure in her new-found happiness she waited silently for the tiny claws, which the other girl had been sharpening on Betty, to be

175

turned upon her. She did not have to wait long.

Sophena slowly lifted her waxen eyelids, revealing a taunting, worldly-wise air of resignation with a glint of malevolence.

"My felicitations. It does not require much experience to see that you and Monsieur have not spent the whole afternoon with an old man!"

Jassy was not to be drawn. Sophena was only guessing after all. She met Sophena's eyes without hesitation and began telling her in a politely detached voice about the pleasant time she had spent with Deshwa Das.

"He's the most fascinating person to talk to."

"But not so fascinating," Sophena's mouth thinned derisively, "as someone else we know." Her shoulders lifted and her hands fluttered out in a flamboyant Gallic shrug. "I pity you, you are so romantic! Ben and I, we are passionate ... but we are realists. I should have known that for him the decision would be realistic, and your wide, adoring eyes must have made it easier. He is a devious devil, that one! I shall enjoy watching this little charade unfold."

Jassy stiffened slightly but continued to look straight at Sophena with cool blankness, determined not to let the fluent spitefulness upset her into giving herself away.

Sophena's green glance hardened. "How could he choose otherwise?" she said with bitter mockery. "Le Grand Seigneur would never endanger his profitable kingdom! Once he had realised you were in love with him it would have been most unwise, most *un*realistic not to use it to his advantage. Just think if you had departed for England full of resentment against him and jealousy of me. With all your valuable inheritance out of his reach!"

Jassy had not shifted her steady gaze, but she could feel the blood draining from her face and it must have been visible to Sophena, for she gave a low gurgle of specious laughter. "*Soit!*" She rose, smoothing the folds of the kaftan. "So be it! I will go now and change for dinner. There is little to do in this tiresome place, but I shall not let myself go to seed for all that."

She lingered another moment, her lips still smiling tightly, pityingly. "Au'voir, *ma chère* Jassy. Make the most of it. Truly he is a wonderful lover, and he will keep you happy long enough for his purpose. Even when he has got what he wants—your shares!—you will still have the consolation of a comfortable home here, if nothing more." She walked airily away, gave a negligent wave from the staircase and went up to her room.

My shares . . . my shares. . . . The words went round and round as Jassy sat quite still, trying to breathe evenly, her hands clasped in her lap with the knuckles going white. She had forgotten those wretched shares. She had felt so safe, been so sure that Sophena no longer had the power to hurt her. But her hour of happiness had been too brief to protect her completely, and she could have wept with dismay at the stabbing shock of uncertainty which had deflated her rapturous mood.

In the days that followed she had to fight hard against the suspicion Sophena had implanted so waspishly. True to his word, Ben said nothing about their unofficial engagement, but every glance, the touch of his hand around her arm, the very tone of his voice was like a caress, and May-lee watched them with a

177

smug, knowing gleam of satisfaction in her eyes.

The birthday celebrations began, first a football match at Main Bay in which the teams played a fast, skilful game in their bare feet, then parties for the children on the islands held at varying times so that Betty could be present at them all. Jassy applied herself with desperately false gaiety to helping Ben run the competitions and races. Afterwards there were feasts spread on long strips of coconut matting under the trees where Betty sat cross-legged among the little ones, loaded with flower garlands as the guest of honour, while Jassy and the other womenfolk did the serving.

On the few occasions she and Ben managed to snatch a moment alone together a guarded tension began to build up in Jassy until it reached a point when she had to force herself to behave naturally. Whenever Ben took her in his arms the emotional insecurity which had dogged her all her life came flooding back, and there was no way she could reason herself out of it. Ben mistook the look of strain. "Tired?" he asked gently, cupping her face in his hands. "You've been doing too much. It'll be easier after the festivities." But she knew it would be more difficult as time went on, and began to panic.

The evening before Betty's actual birthday, after they had had coffee in the *salle*, he rose and, stretching a hand out to Jassy, said with a serious, almost businesslike abstraction : "I've been working on some-thing lately which I'd like to discuss with you. Come into the office."

Reluctantly she followed him to the turret room. It was a practical, impersonal work-room, furnished with

178

a large desk and upright chairs in African iroko wood, books lining the whole of the inner wall from the ceiling to the red-tiled floor, large-scale Admiralty charts and a bank of steel-grey radio equipment. In spite of the warm air Jassy shivered a little, remembering that first, unexpected *frisson* of desire when he had kissed her here.

He turned purposefully towards her, but she evaded his arms and said hurriedly: "What did you want to talk to me about?"

He cocked a quizzical eyebrow but went round the desk and picked up a sheaf of brownish, inscribed parchment. "I've been going through the family Articles and drafting some figures for a scheme for your shares."

"My shares...." Jassy's heart leapt, stopped, then began again in slow heavy strokes.

"If we can get it sorted out and agreed before we're married the lawyers can start organising the changes without delay."

"Yes," was all she could force out. *Sophena was right*, she thought blankly. But I feel nothing. Why do I feel nothing? What's happening to me?

Ben was disconcerted by the expressionless gaze which looked right through him. "For the love of Mike, what now? I thought you were anxious to have this awkward business settled. Well, I've found a way. Do you want to hear the details?" He stiffened watchfully. "Not exactly falling over yourself with enthusiasm, are you, Jassy?"

The flick of sarcasm goaded her into a stir of renewed feeling, confirming the fears Sophena had implanted. She had to bring her doubts into the open

179

now, whatever the cost, pouring out her humiliation in a small, cold voice.

"Ben, are you marrying me for my shares? There's no need. As far as I'm concerned the shares are yours by rights already. I don't want to go on with this farce. In London I could see a good lawyer, someone who can find a loophole in the Articles which would make it all legal and let me out."

The astonishment in his face gave way to disbelief, then to a flaring anger. She drew a sharp breath. "You're trying to protect the Islands, Ben, I understand how you feel. This physical attraction makes it easier for you, but not for me. It will pass and I . . . I can't live with it."

"Do you realise what you're implying?" Ben caught her wrists in a vicelike grip sending pain shooting up her arms. "That I'm a cynical opportunist like Taylor, using you to suit my own purpose? My God, you're questioning my integrity!" His eyes were black, blazing with fury. "You don't understand how I feel, Jassy, you never will. You've made up your squalid little mind!"

He thrust her aside with such forceful repugnance that she fell into a chair, trembling with regret and a sickening conviction that under his scathing fury he was deeply hurt. Before she could stammer out an abject apology he swung round again, stiff and obdurate.

"We can't build a relationship for the rest of our lives without trust, Jassy." Picking up the documents, he threw them into a drawer and locked it. "How right you were about not making a premature announcement! For Betty's sake try and keep things

180

going, and I'll have a word with Ray Calver about your flight arrangements to London as soon as I can."

"Thank you," she whispered, dazed by the sudden collapse of all her secret hopes for reassurance and love. Pride was all she had left : pride to match his. She left the room, moving like a puppet with no further life of her own.

Next morning Betty was inundated with lovingly made hand embroideries, wood carvings and tortoiseshell trinkets. Jassy gave her the little make-up box she had been hoarding, and Ben's gift was a superbly matched string of pearls. In an enormous parcel from Ray, under layer upon layer of paper, Betty found a bright pink sugar-lollipop. "I'll *kill* him!" she gasped, choking with laughter.

Ben disappeared with Tao after breakfast, but only Tao returned in time to take them to Main Bay in the launch; Jassy in flowing, rustling ivory taffeta, Betty in her butterfly blue and silver gown, her pony-tail pinned up in a pretty coronet of tasselling curls, her face flushed with happiness. As they crossed the green Jassy took a hold on herself to get through the long evening.

The lounge of the guest-house had been transformed into a bower of flowers and greenery sparkling with a tracery of coloured lights. Ben was nowhere to be seen, but Ray came to meet them, very ceremonious in his white dress uniform.

"Wow!" he said. "You're like a creamy, exotic orchid tonight, Jassy-gal!"

"And *me*?" cried the small, crestfallen voice at her side. "Ra-a-y?"

Jassy saw the flicker of pain in his face. He moved close to Betty, gazing down into her anxious, self-conscious eyes, and said huskily: "You look so beautiful, love, I think I must be dreaming. A happy birthday, half-pint." He began searching clumsily in his pockets. Jassy knew it was his real gift this time and seeing the looks on both their faces turned away and left them together.

Within half an hour the lounge was full of people, the murmur of conversation, and chink of ice against glasses, and rich, hazy fragrance of Burmese cheroots. The men were in white evening dress or high-necked, knee-length black linen coats, the women in rainbow gossamer *saris* or shot-silk sarongs. May-lee sailed round the room like a galleon, magnificent in solferino satin, Miss Jones wore a dowdy black gown she had probably had for years, and Miss Millie and Miss Mary were almost identically dressed in shades of pale grey.

Shortly before dinner was announced Sophena made an entrance, almost floating down the staircase in a froth of cerise chiffon and sequins. Her eyes were sulky, her laughter bored and brittle. So Ben had not been with her after all! thought Jassy, her spirits rising a little. But still, no sign of him . . . where could he be? No one commented on his absence.

Then he appeared, towering tall, impeccably groomed in a white dress suit. He wheeled in the cane bath-chair. He had fetched Deshwa Das to the party.

With a squeal of pleasure Betty ran forward to welcome D.D., but Jassy stayed well in the background, discreetly avoiding Ben as he went round greeting the guests. When she entered the dining-room with Mr Chandra and took her place at one of the two long, decorated tables she suddenly came face to face with Ben. The enigmatic look, travelling over her from head to toe, made her flush and bite her lip. He wheeled D.D.'s chair in beside her, then walked away to his own seat at the head of the table.

Recovering as best she could, she bent towards the old man, met the disarming twinkle in his eyes and said sincerely; "I'm so glad you could come."

"My health has improved. Betty's coming-of-age is very close to our hearts, I could not miss this important occasion." He pushed the fine Kashmir shawl back from his shoulders. "I wished to see you again too, Jacynth, to talk over my plan." Turning to an attentive waiter he said : "No, I will take only some tonic water and dry toast, thank you."

Jassy chose the deliciously spicy pickled eggs in preference to chilled melon. "What plan is that?" she asked with a fixed smile, wondering how she would last out without breaking down in ignominious tears.

"Perhaps Ben has not yet had time to explain my proposal for putting your shares into a trust fund for the Suran people?"

His gentle question gave her a shock. She was dismayed. Her hand shook; she put her fork down. "*A trust fund*? I . . . we . . . we didn't really discuss it."

"Oh? Why was that? You do not care to sell to us?"

She could not speak for a moment. In a stifled voice she confessed : "D.D., I made a terrible mistake and we didn't get that far. Would you tell me now?"

Had she been aware of anything but her own confusion she would have seen the perceptive look on his withered face. He waited as she was served with tastily garnished fillet of pomfret specially flown in on ice for the banquet.

"Ah, well!" he said. "You know, Jacynth, Ben visits me almost every day, and I have guessed for some time from the way he spoke of you that he wanted you for his wife. I could not understand at first why there should be any difficulty, it seemed an ideal arrangement. Ben conceded after a while that he did not think your regard for him went beyond friendship, but when you came to my house, I knew you loved him as he loved you. Am I right?"

She agreed faintly, sipping some wine, and left her fish half finished.

"Soon I saw Ben was in good spirits : I concluded that you and he had come to terms. And yet he was still restless. Something was preying on his mind—which I put to him persistently until he admitted that your shares were troubling him. He is a proud man, Jacynth, and would not accept your shares as a matter of right by marriage. He wished you to have their value in money to give you a sense of independence after the shabby behaviour of your guardians. He couldn't urge you to sell to strangers, nor could he raise the capital himself. *Impasse!*" he remarked dryly. "When I had thought this over, and consulted other friends, I proposed to Ben that the Advisory Council should set up a trust fund to which every Suran could contribute to buy your shares on your marriage. Ben decided to study the Lanyard Articles and draft a trust deed which would endow the ordinary people of the islands with share-holdings; in fact the plan appealed to him so strongly he offered to put all his resources into the trust too. What we require is your consent, Jacynth."

"Oh, D.D.!—and I wouldn't even listen to him!" She was distressed. "Anyway, I'd never accept any money as Ben's wife, never! I'll only consent if I can *give* you my shares for the trust!" Her voice faltered. "But it's too late."

"My dear child, don't upset yourself," he sighed. "Did you quarrel with Ben?"

She nodded miserably. "Believe it or not, I practically accused him of marrying me for my sh-shares!" She gripped her hands hard in her lap as she was served with steak, savoury tomato rice and tiny, crisp fried rings of okra.

"You Lanyards," Deshwa Das smiled with wry humour, "too strongwilled and stiffnecked for your own good! He with his scruples about your inheritance and you with your prickly pride. Forgive an old man interfering, but I know Ben; if you have doubted his love and integrity you must make the first move, Jacynth."

"You think he might be willing?"

"I know," he assured her quietly, and turned to speak to his other neighbour.

Jassy tackled the steak without appetite, her mind in a whirl. The sound of cutlery and buzz of voices billowed round her, leaving her isolated. Somewhere inside her hope had begun to stir, then shyness and the old fear of being rejected almost quenched it again. She would try and approach Ben after dinner . . . no, too many people around . . . tomorrow perhaps, if he gave her an opportunity . . . if! What was she eating? Steak?—more like veal or venison. What did it matter? Nothing mattered, except Ben. She looked up involuntarily and found him watching her from the head of the table, a devilish glint in his eye. He looked at her plate and she knew instantly what she was eating. Turtle ... *turtle steak*! ... She made a shaky effort to smile and hurried into a conversation with Mr Chandra on her left, deluging him with a spate of absent-minded chatter for the rest of the meal and refusing the colourful almond, orange and pistachio desserts.

When the huge birthday cake had been wheeled in, glowing with candles, and Betty had cut it, speeches were made, toasts were drunk and Betty replied with an enchanting bashfulness which conveyed more than her halting words. In the lounge again, green and cool as a cave, the little lights winked festively and the air pulsed with soft, rhythmic music from a record player. The centre had been cleared and Betty was swept out on to the polished boards by the young Suran pilot, Ramu. Jassy was soon claimed by Ray and Sophena got up rather pettishly to dance with Jimmy Renton. Concentrating on the older guests, Ben moved from one little table to the next. He was an urbane, very attractive host, occasionally persuading one of the Suran ladies to dance sedately with him. But before long they left the floor to the exuberant younger ones.

Coffee was served and liqueurs. The evening stretched interminably before Jassy until she saw the delight Betty radiated at her first grown-up party and felt guilty about her own fretful, self-centred moping. She glimpsed Ben once with Sophena, but from the expression on the girl's face and the peevish way she was fussing with her hair and dress it was obvious

Ben's conversation didn't please her. Gradually Jassy became calmer, and even began to enjoy herself as she went from partner to partner and allowed herself to be drawn into the talk and laughter with a growing consciousness of being part of this friendly island community. If only Ben had shown a little interest, asked her to dance. . . .

She was about to sink into a chair while one of the young men fetched her an iced drink when Ben came up from the next table. On the spur of the moment she took a step towards him and smiled straight into his narrowed eyes.

"Ben, it's a lovely party—Betty's so happy!"

She held her breath for a response, however small. Without a word he grasped her hand and pulled her to him, slid an arm round her waist and took her out on the dance floor. For minutes she was speechless, her feet going instinctively with the rhythm, her heart thudding against the hard, lean length of him.

Through a wave of relief she heard him say in an ironic undertone: "I thought I'd have to introduce a *cipaye* into the room to get you into my arms again."

"Oh, Ben!"—it was the first break in the stony wall of rejection. Jassy clutched his sleeve and ventured nervously: "Ben, I've been talking to D.D."

"So I observed," was the laconic reply.

"He told me all about the trust . . . it's a wonderful idea, isn't it?"

"Is it?" he said offhandedly.

"I think it is," she rushed on blindly, "except that I'm going to give them my shares, not sell. When we're m-married I can do that, c-can't I?"

"When *you're* married—you could," he countered

pointedly.

Her hopes plummeted and she turned white. "What can I say?" she pleaded wretchedly. "I'm so ashamed I'll never forgive myself. I can't think what came over me, letting Sophena get under my skin like that—"

"Sophena?" his arm contracted sharply.

"It doesn't matter," she murmured. The pleasure and poignancy of being crushed up to him raced in her veins like fire, though the taut pressure was punishing enough to have cracked her ribs.

"Ben," there was a catch in her throat, "you didn't m-mean it the other night . . . about s-sending me away."

"What makes you so sure?" His tone was still a cold dead-level, refusing to help her out.

She looked up slowly, right up into the inflexible lines of his face. An exultant feeling of reprieve shot through her as she recognised that dark, piercing intensity in his eyes and the rigid way he was holding her.

She said very softly: "Because I didn't mean a word of what I said either, and I'm truly sorry. You should have kissed me or beaten me or something!" No answer. He was demanding more; complete capitulation. Pressing herself against him, willing his rigid body to yield, she whispered: "Because I love you so much I can't live without you now."

He stopped abruptly in the middle of the dance floor, released her hand and locked her in his arms.

"Ben, not here!" she exclaimed, her cheeks burning with embarrassment.

"Here and now!" he said trenchantly. "Do you think I'm made of stone? We love each other and the sooner everybody knows the better. Say : yes, Ben."

"Yes, Ben. . . ." she said dizzily.

"You've put me through the hoop twice—never again !"

"Ben, you're hurting, I can't breathe !"

"Never doubt me again, my darling, or I'll wring your pretty little neck !"

"Yes, Ben," she shivered ecstatically as his hand enclosed her throat.

The room had suddenly gone silent, the other couples had deserted the dance floor. Without daring to look Jassy could feel the surprise and curiosity and warmth of expectant smiles in the hush surrounding them.

Ben's caressing hand came up, lifting her face to his. "Well ?" the muscle twitched beside his mouth. "Our audience is waiting, and so am I. Shall I kiss you now?" The tender laughter sprang into his eyes. "Say : yes, Ben."

For a second she hesitated. But this was the love of her life; and these were her friends, her people. She belonged here. She had come home at last ! A tide of joy swept her inhibitions away.

With his breath on her lips she said : "Yes . . . please, Ben."

Each month from Harlequin

8 NEW FULL LENGTH ROMANCE NOVELS

Listed below are the last three months' releases:

1929	COLLISION COURSE, Jane Donnelly
1930	WEB OF SILVER, Lucy Gillen
1931	LULLABY OF LEAVES, Janice Gray
1932	THE KISSING GATE, Joyce Dingwell
1933	MISS NOBODY FROM NOWHERE, Elizabeth Ashton
1934	A STRANGER IS MY LOVE, Margaret Malcolm
1935	THAT MAN BRYCE, Mary Wibberley
1936	REMEMBERED SERENADE, Mary Burchell
1937	HENRIETTA'S OWN CASTLE, Betty Neels
1938	SWEET SANCTUARY, Charlotte Lamb
1939	THE GIRL AT DANES' DYKE, Margaret Rome
1940	THE SYCAMORE SONG, Elizabeth Hunter
1941	LOVE AND THE KENTISH MAID, Betty Beaty
1942	THE FIRE AND THE FURY, Rebecca Stratton
1943	THE GARDEN OF DREAMS, Sara Craven
1944	HEART IN THE SUNLIGHT, Lilian Peake
1945	THE DESERT CASTLE, Isobel Chace
1946	CROWN OF WILLOW, Elizabeth Ashton
1947	THE GIRL IN THE BLUE DRESS, Mary Burchell
1948	ROSS OF SILVER RIDGE, Gwen Westwood
1949	SHINING WANDERER, Rose Elver
1950	THE BEACH OF SWEET RETURNS, Margery Hilton
1951	RIDE A BLACK HORSE, Margaret Pargeter
1952	CORPORATION BOSS, Joyce Dingwell

75c each

These titles are available at your local bookseller, or through the Harlequin Reader Service, M.P.O. Box 707, Niagara Falls, N.Y. 14302; Canadian address 649 Ontario St., Stratford, Ont. N5A 6W4.

Have You Missed Any of These

Harlequin Romances?

All books listed 75¢

Harlequin Romances are available at your local bookseller, or through the Harlequin Reader Service, M.P.O. Box 707, Niagara Falls, N.Y. 14302; Canadian address: 649 Ontario St., Stratford, Ontario N5A 6W4.

Have You Missed Any of These
Harlequin Romances?

☐ 1905 TABITHA IN MOONLIGHT,
Betty Neels
☐ 1906 TAKE BACK YOUR LOVE,
Katrina Britt
☐ 1907 ENCHANTMENT IN BLUE,
Flora Kidd
☐ 1908 A TOUCH OF HONEY,
Lucy Gillen
☐ 1909 THE SHIFTING SANDS,
Kay Thorpe
☐ 1910 CANE MUSIC, Joyce Dingwell
☐ 1911 STORMY HARVEST,
Janice Gray
☐ 1912 THE SPANISH INHERITANCE,
Elizabeth Hunter
☐ 1913 THE FLIGHT OF THE HAWK,
Rebecca Stratton
☐ 1914 FLOWERS IN STONY PLACES,
Marjorie Lewty
☐ 1915 EAST TO BARRYVALE,
Yvonne Whittal
☐ 1916 WHEELS OF CONFLICT,
Sue Peters

☐ 1917 ANNA OF STRATHALLAN,
Essie Summers
☐ 1918 THE PLAYER KING,
Elizabeth Ashton
☐ 1919 JUST A NICE GIRL,
Mary Burchell
☐ 1920 HARBOUR OF DECEIT,
Roumelia Lane
☐ 1921 HEAVEN IS GENTLE,
Betty Neels
☐ 1922 COTSWOLD HONEY,
Doris E. Smith
☐ 1923 ALWAYS A RAINBOW,
Gloria Bevan
☐ 1924 THE DARK ISLE,
Mary Wibberley
☐ 1925 BEWARE THE HUNTSMAN,
Sophie Weston
☐ 1926 THE VOICE IN THE
THUNDER, Elizabeth Hunter
☐ 1927 WANDALILLI PRINCESS
Dorothy Cork
☐ 1928 GENTLE TYRANT, Lucy Gillen

All books listed are available at **75c each** at your local bookseller or through the Harlequin Reader Service.